HAPPY *EVEN* AFTER

RAY HOBBS

Wingspan Press

Published in the United States and the United Kingdom
by WingSpan Press, Livermore, CA

The WingSpan name, logo and colophon are the trademarks
of WingSpan Publishing.

ISBN 978-1-59594-648-5 (pbk.)
ISBN 978-1-59594-960-8 (ebk.)

First edition 2020

Printed in the United States of America

www.wingspanpress.com

1 2 3 4 5 6 7 8 9 10

'I want a happily even after. The kind of happiness you have to earn. The kind you find after a broken heart or an injured knee…. It's the even after part that matters.' —Kami Garcia.

This book is dedicated to music-loving and gardening Aberdeen terriers past, present and as yet unplanned....

Acknowledgements

My thanks are due to my late and greatly-missed companion Phoebe for the photograph on the back cover.

I also wish to acknowledge the advice of my brother Chris, whose knowledge of academic institutions, whilst not specifically of the kind described in the following pages, is more recent than mine.

Author's Note
For Readers Outside the UK

It occurs to me that describing traditional British pantomime to a non-British readership is somewhat akin to explaining the offside rule in football, the leg-before-wicket rule in cricket or, for that matter, cricket itself. However, the pioneering spirit lives on, and I shall nerve myself to make the effort. Otherwise, the goings-on in Freddy's pantomime will remain, for some, an eternal mystery.

This kind of pantomime owes nothing to classical theatrical mime, but is a musical play for children, performed at Christmas and usually based on a fairy tale or folk legend. The hero, or 'principal boy', is played by a young woman. The 'dame', a plain and elderly but comical woman, is played by a man. There is usually a good fairy, played by a woman, and a bad fairy, witch or demon played by a person of either sex, as no one is likely to find him or her remotely attractive anyway.

The pantomime Dick Whittington is based very loosely, and usually with unbounded licence, on the true story of Richard Whittington, a 14th century merchant, who became Lord Mayor of London three times and married Alice, the daughter of Alderman Fitzwarren. Those are the historical facts, but there the resemblance to the true story ends.

In any pantomime, there is much slapstick comedy; a messy kitchen scene is favourite, featuring the dame and the comic butt of the pantomime, usually a young man. In other scenes, vocal participation by the audience is encouraged.

The whole experience sounds like a cross-dressing extravaganza, but it is simply good, clean family fun, and I heartily recommend it.

RH

1

AUGUST 1975
NIDDERDALE, NORTH YORKSHIRE

Leah opened her eyes, blinking until her vision cleared. She hadn't intended falling asleep; daytime napping was never a good idea, as she would probably remind herself later. Lying awake in the middle of the night was one feature of hospital routine that she looked forward to leaving behind.

She lay still for a while, studying the print that hung on the wall opposite, not that there was much to study. It was simply a fair representation of a bowl of violets. Flowers were a feature in hospital rooms; there was a vase full of them on a little wall table, left there as a gesture of sympathy or maybe as a warning against hospital blues. Possibly, they were saying, 'You think you've got problems with your knee, girlie. We've had our legs amputated, and now we have to stand in water 'til we die and get chucked on to the compost heap.' It was a salutary reminder, and she was making an effort to be cheerful about nothing in particular, when one of the nurses looked in.

'I just popped in to make sure you were decent, Leah. You have a visitor.'

'Lovely.' She'd no idea who it might be, although she was expecting her parents later.

The door opened wider to admit the visitor.

'Hello, Leah.'

'Vincent, you lovely man!'

Vincent Palmer, Head of Drama and Dance and therefore Leah's boss, deposited a box of Terry's All Gold chocolates on her bedside table.

'I thought you'd have enough flowers, so I brought you these,' he said.

'Bless you, Vincent,' she said, offering her cheek, 'although I'll need to go on a diet when I get out of this place.'

'Your slender figure will stand it, my dear.' His voice was deep and resonant. 'But you've had something done to those delectable chestnut locks.' Not surprisingly in the circumstances, she was wearing her hair down, but it was now off the shoulder.

'I've only had it cut to make it manageable in hospital, but it's kind of you to tell me that.' It was also typical of him. 'Thank you for your card as well, Vincent. A kind gesture makes a huge difference when the next pain-killer is two hours away.'

'I'm glad it helps.' He drew up a chair and sat down. He wore flared jeans and a black T-shirt decorated with an obscure emblem. His fair hair was caught in a ponytail, and his manner was sincere. 'How are you feeling now?'

'It's improving,' she said. 'I'm told I have to be patient.'

'But was the operation successful?'

'They say so. I mean, we have to be realistic and advise Dame Margot not to rush into retirement, but I'll be okay.'

'I know, Leah. It means an awful lot to you.'

She patted his hand lightly. 'My dream went up in smoke eight years ago with the accident, Vincent. I'm happy now if I can go on teaching dance.'

'I'm sure you can.' He gave her an encouraging smile, and asked, 'Where would we be without you?'

'You'd find someone else.'

'Your shoes would be hard to fill, but let's not think about that.'

'It's better not to,' she agreed.

He peered at the card from her parents and her brother, and asked, 'Are you the only dancer in your family?'

'No, my mum's done lots of dancing. She never turned professional, but I suppose she was overtaken by events, mainly the war.' She smiled suddenly, and said, 'My dad's pet name for her is "SP".'

'Her initials?'

'One of them is, but it actually stands for "Sugar Plum", as in the fairy of that confection.'

'I'm intrigued.'

'Okay.' She made herself comfortable against her pillows, and began. 'She wrote to him when he was a prisoner-of-war in Poland, and told him about a ballet presentation she was in when she was very young. Although she didn't realise it, she was going down with 'flu or some such thing at the time, and she was, according to her, the worst Sugar Plum Fairy ever. However, since that letter, he's only ever addressed her as "SP".'

He was about to comment on the story, when a nurse put her head round the door to ask, 'Would either of you like a cup of tea or something?'

'How very kind,' said Vincent.

'We'd both like tea, please,' said Leah, knowing that Vincent never drank anything else in the afternoon.

'Milk, but no sugar, please,' said Vincent.

'Right you are.' The nurse left them.

'I must say, this hospital is very nice,' said Vincent.

'It is. In the ordinary way, I'd have waited and gone into an NHS hospital,' she explained, 'but my dad insisted I came in here and had the operation straight away.' She smiled again. 'He's funny, you know.'

'In what sense?'

'He made all kinds of excuses when he took out private health insurance for the family, being the idealist he is, but I suppose he thought it was necessary, being self-employed. Mind you, he's let it be known far and wide that he'll never vote Labour now that they've killed off the Fleet Air Arm. At the same time, though, he'll never vote for the other lot as long as they're led by what he calls "a stormtrooper with a handbag".'

The door opened and the same nurse came in carrying a tray.

'Oh, lovely,' said Leah. 'Thank you very much.'

'Yes,' said Vincent, 'that's very kind of you. Thank you.'

'Not at all.'

When the nurse was gone, Vincent asked, 'Was your dad in the Fleet Air Arm?'

'Yes, he was an air-gunner until he was taken prisoner.' She accepted a cup of tea and a biscuit.

'And did he and your mum know each other before that?'

'No, the story goes that my dad was at a low ebb because he'd lost all his family in the bombing of Hull, and his POW friend Len wrote to his wife, who was serving in the Wrens, and asked if she had a pal who could write to him. Now, her best friend was my mum, who'd also lost someone. I only found out quite recently that she'd had a boyfriend, a sailor who was killed at sea, and Auntie Joyce – that's Uncle Len's wife – thought it would be good for both of them. That's how it all began.'

'And their relationship took off from there?'

'That's right. It just gathered momentum, so that they were crazy about each other long before they met.'

'How marvellous.'

'Yes,' she said, taking another biscuit, 'that's the way they do things, the romantic way.' Just looking at Vincent reminded her of something important and not at all romantic. She asked, 'Have you seen the inspector's report yet, Vincent?'

'Yes.'

She gathered from his tone, that the report wasn't all good news. Even so, she put her cup down and prepared to hear the worst.

'We came out of it okay. You got a good write-up, and the drama staff were highly-praised as well.'

'But not the Music School, presumably?'

'You presume correctly. There were exceptions but, generally speaking, they were criticised for their ossified teaching styles and entrenched attitudes, to name only two of their shortcomings. It's not the advertisement we've been looking for to improve student numbers, and it's not going to impress the CNAA either.'

'The who?'

'The Council for National Academic Awards, the body that would validate our degree courses if they were ever allowed to become reality.'

'Oh, glory.' It was going to take more than a vase of cut flowers to keep her spirits up.

'And unless we can increase student numbers, the likelihood is that the college will close.' He smiled apologetically. 'I didn't come here to depress you,' he said, 'but I suspect I have.'

'No, we have to be realistic.' Her mind went back to the last departmental meeting she'd attended, and she asked, 'Did anything come of your idea to mount a show by way of advertisement?'

He nodded. 'Neil's working on it.'

'Oh.' Neil Quarmby wasn't one of Leah's favourite colleagues.

'Be fair, Leah. He has some good ideas.'

'It's just as well. We're going to need them.'

'And a great deal will depend on the new music lecturer, always supposing they manage to appoint one.' His expression lacked confidence.

'Is there a problem with that?'

'There shouldn't be, but Dr Francis has gone on long-term sick leave, so Jonathan Best is currently in charge over there.'

Leah closed her eyes in a gesture of hopelessness. 'And he could pour cold water on anyone's enthusiasm,' she said. 'I suppose it's too much to hope that he'll be away on holiday when they hold the interviews.'

2

SEPTEMBER

Jonathan Best had grey, tousled eyebrows, a veined complexion, and a permanent air of disillusionment. He looked like a man accustomed to receiving and imparting bad news.

'It's a shame I wasn't available when they interviewed you,' he said. 'As it happened, I was having my hernia repaired. It was very necessary.' His tone suggested that, far from being a nuisance, the operation had been a welcome diversion from work. 'I imagine the interview panel brushed all the problems under the carpet. They usually do.'

'They must have hidden them somewhere,' said Gavin, 'although, in the circumstances, I didn't exactly do much probing.' He'd gone as far as reading the inspector's report on the college, and particularly the Music School, and he'd found it less than complimentary, with quite a lot to say about low staff morale, a feature Jonathan was now demonstrating most ably. Whatever misgivings Gavin might have had, however, the inescapable truth was that he'd taken the job because he needed it.

'The rot set in, you know, when they let the Benton-on-Ouse lot in.'

'The drama college?'

Jonathan nodded. 'Did they explain all that at your interview?'

'Not in any depth.'

'I'll give you a potted history, then. The situation was that their building was falling apart, and they approached the Trust about the possibility of accommodation here. In the end, the Trust agreed to a merger, and the establishment became known as Nidderdale College of Performance Arts.' He gestured with his thumb through the window behind him. 'The Drama School is housed in the old coach house, stables and various temporary buildings. This building,' he said with territorial smugness, 'was Boothroyd Hall, the house built by the Boothroyd family in the nineteenth century.'

'Right, so both schools are governed by the Trust?'

'Yes, the Board of Administrators of the Boothroyd Trust, to give it its full title. Sir William Boothroyd was a local silk manufacturer, who left a pile of money, as well as the Hall, for the provision of a school of music in Nidderdale, and the poor bugger must be turning in his grave.'

A certificate on the wall to Jonathan's left, stated that he was a Fellow of the Royal College of Organists, and it occurred to Gavin that it was the first time he'd heard an organist swear. He welcomed the irony, because his spirits needed a lift, even a modest one.

'At one time,' Jonathan went on, 'the Trust was administered by people who knew what the job was about, and this place produced some damned good musicians, but now the Board consists largely of accountants and lawyers, none of whom knows a fart from an A flat, and who've made one lamentable decision after another.' He winced as he recalled an example. 'Their latest aberration is the Foundation Course with the Popular Music Option. Have you seen the syllabus?'

'Yes, I have. Are you saying it's a mistake?'

'It's an unmitigated disaster, but the Trust decided it was worth pursuing, largely because it attracts government funding and because certain other establishments have made the mistake of going down that path, and we must naturally compete with them for students.'

'When does the course begin?'

'At the start of the coming term. That's when we shall have our first intake of three-chord guitarists with colossal egos and sod-all ability, all waiting for some TV talent show to catapult them into stardom.' His face took on a rigid look, and it seemed, just for a few seconds, that he might have suffered a stroke, but he spoke again. 'I ask you,' he said weakly, 'what will they inflict on us next?' His grimace subsided, and he said, 'I'll take you across to the Drama School. They want to talk to you, but I should warn you that a young, good-looking, fair-haired chap like you is bound to cause excitement over there, so watch out.'

Gavin wondered a little about Jonathan's view of the world and its inhabitants. He'd never thought of himself as good-looking, and his hair was too dark to be called 'fair'. He was twenty-seven, so he could be described as young, but he didn't believe for one moment that the drama school was populated by gay predators. Patiently, he picked up his coat and followed his superior into the oak-lined corridor.

When they came to the office of the Secretary to Dr William Francis, Head of the Music School, Jonathan tapped on the door and pushed it open. A neatly-dressed woman, possibly in her forties, sat at her desk typing.

'Good morning, Maggie.'

'Good morning, Jonathan.'

'This is Gavin Lowe, the new Senior Lecturer. I'm taking him across to Fairyland, so wish him luck.'

'Don't be silly.' She shook Gavin's hand. 'How do you do, Gavin? Take no notice of this curmudgeon.'

'I'll try not to,' he assured her. 'Glad to meet you, Maggie.'

As they walked on, Gavin, who had yet to meet the Head of School, asked, 'Has Dr Francis been ill for long?'

'Since June. It's his nerves, you know. It gets them all like that eventually.'

'I'd like to think you're exaggerating, but something tells me you're not.'

'Not in the least. My predecessor took early retirement with a duodenal ulcer, and I'd follow his example if I could develop something sufficiently convincing. Otherwise, I'll have to settle for normal retirement in a year's time.' He gave a rare, faint smile, possibly counting the weeks.

As they left the building and walked in the welcome sunshine, Jonathan asked, 'Are you married?'

'No.'

'Very wise.' Gavin could almost have beaten him to the line.

He looked around him at the generously-proportioned outbuildings, wondering about the wealth of the man who had created the estate.

They came to a large, square building with a sign confirming that they had arrived at the Drama and Dance School, and they entered a spacious foyer that led to a pair of doors signed *Theatre*. A young woman with fair, feather-cut hair was about to enter an office off the foyer, when Jonathan greeted her.

'Good morning, Clare. Vincent's expecting us.'

'One moment, Jonathan. I'll find out what he's doing.' She disappeared into the office, returning a few moments later to say, 'He'll be with you shortly. He's on the phone.' She re-entered the office, leaving the door open, and Gavin noticed a vase of dahlias on the windowsill. There were also two large potted plants in the foyer that he couldn't identify, but which were no less welcoming.

'The place is quiet now,' said Jonathan, 'but just wait until the end of the month. You won't be able to move for students practising their *pliés*, striking poses and calling each other "darling".'

Gavin saw Clare raise a resentful eyebrow. He couldn't blame her, and he was relieved when the inner door opened, and the occupant of the office emerged. His jeans, T-shirt and ponytail set him apart immediately from Jonathan.

'Jonathan,' he said in a deep, sonorous voice, 'I'm sorry to have kept you waiting. I see you've brought the new chap.'

'That's right, Vincent. This is Gavin Lowe. Gavin, meet Vincent Palmer, Head of the Drama School.'

'Drama *and Dance* School,' Vincent corrected him as he shook Gavin's hand.

'I have to leave you, I'm afraid,' said Jonathan. 'I have some time-tabling hitches to attend to.'

'In that case, don't let us keep you.'

Jonathan gave them a cursory wave and departed, leaving Gavin to rectify an omission.

'We haven't been introduced, Clare,' he said. 'I'm Gavin.'

She smiled and shook his hand. 'Glad to meet you, Gavin.' Then, as Vincent opened the door to his office, she turned and asked, 'Do you need anything, Vincent?'

'Just coffee and protection, dearest, if you please.'

'Consider them yours.'

'You're an angel.' He beckoned Gavin into his office. 'I beg your pardon, Gavin,' he said. 'I should have asked you if you preferred tea or coffee.'

'Coffee will be very welcome, thank you.'

'That girl is pure gold, Gavin,' he said, offering him a seat, 'and her husband's a hulking great builder. Some people have all the luck. All the same, you probably made a useful ally with that little gesture.'

'It was more than a gesture, Vincent. I don't like to see anyone excluded.'

'Nor I, Gavin. I've no doubt you've heard a few negative remarks about us this morning.'

'I really shouldn't comment.'

'You don't need to. I'm afraid Jonathan holds us all in very low esteem.' He shrugged. 'But tell me about yourself. You were at Rossington College, I believe. Such a tragedy it has to close.'

'I can't disagree with that. It's the reason I'm here.'

'Quite, and now you have to make the best of what you see around you, but try not to be downhearted. The glory days of the Music School are behind us, as you've no doubt heard, but there is potential here if Jonathan and a few others will only be a little more receptive.' He stopped when Clare came in with the coffee things.

'I know Neil's on his way to join you, so I brought an extra cup,' she said, placing the tray on the low coffee table between them.

'Thank you, Clare. You're ahead of me, as usual.'

When they were alone again, he said, 'I imagine Jonathan's told you about his *bête noire.*'

'The Foundation Course?'

'Yes.' He poured coffee into two cups. 'What are your feelings about it?'

Gavin considered his answer, distracted for the moment by the novelty of coffee served in a china cup and saucer rather than the usual workplace mug. 'I think the Foundation Course is necessary,' he said, 'and we have to cater for popular demand.'

'A careful reply.' Vincent smiled approvingly.

'No, I mean it. It's a genuine opportunity for students who want to give post-sixteen school education a miss and go straight into music education. It's also a means of subsidising conventional courses, and the Pop Music Option, which is Jonathan's real bug-bear, does mean that some of tomorrow's recording stars will actually be able to play their instruments instead of having to rely on session musicians to do it for them.'

'And it's a means of staying afloat.'

'I imagine so.'

'The situation is more critical than you may think, Gavin. Student numbers are tumbling. We are no longer the popular choice.' Before he could say more, there was a knock on the office door.

'Come.'

The man who stepped into the office resembled an eager mail-order model. He wore flared, designer jeans with trainers, and a T-shirt that proclaimed his allegiance to Earth, Wind and Fire. His dark hair was down to the shoulder and blow-combed into waves.

'Neil,' said Vincent, 'and right on cue for once.'

'I'm always on cue, you old teaser.' The newcomer laughed with exaggerated bonhomie.

'Come in and meet Gavin.'

'Delighted.' He turned to Gavin as if seeing him for the first time, and extended his hand with an elegant flourish.

'Neil Quarmby, Senior Lecturer in Drama, this is Gavin Lowe, Senior Lecturer in Music with responsibility for Composition.'

'Gavin.' Neil spoke the name like a connoisseur recalling a fine vintage. 'What a blissfully rugged name.' He took Gavin's hand in a loose clasp.

'How d' you do?' Gavin was unimpressed.

'Believe it or not, Gavin,' said Vincent, 'beneath the camp act, which inevitably goes down well with the more naïve and impressionable students, Neil is as straight as any of us.'

'I see.' The man's sexual inclination meant nothing to Gavin, but his posing was downright irritating.

'It's a pity Leah can't join us,' said Vincent.

'Oh, isn't she here?' Neil looked around him unnecessarily.

'She'll be in later.' For Gavin's benefit, he explained, 'Leah is our dance *suprema*, but she had a hospital appointment today. The poor girl had a knee operation recently. She only joined us in January, but she's a valuable asset.'

'But not at all keen on men,' said Neil pointedly.

'Don't be so bitchy, Neil,' said Vincent. 'Have you brought the script?'

'It's 'ere in me 'ot little 'and.' He placed a manila folder on the coffee table.

'This, said Vincent, tapping the folder, 'given the right kind of media coverage, is the musical that we hope will revive our flagging fortunes and enable our survival. Do you think Gavin might see the blurb, Neil?'

'No sooner said than done, milord.' Neil lifted the flap and took out a single sheet of paper, which he handed to Gavin with the inevitable flourish.

Feeling that he had no choice, Gavin read the summary.

Royal Rivals
Or
A Throne of Contention

The play is set in The Hereafter, where earthly rank counts for nothing and wealth is an impediment. The crowned heads of history are accommodated in one of the Lower Chambers, happy enough for much of the time, but they dream occasionally of life in the Upper Chambers, home of the heroes, heroines and great minds of the centuries, who enjoy the ungrudging respect of the entire community.

An official messenger arrives with startling news. Thanks to a hard-hitting piece of investigative journalism, a hero has been debunked, thus vacating a place in one of the Upper Chambers. It has been decided that it is the turn of royal personages to be considered and, for the first time in many years, each monarch is invited to make his or her pitch for promotion. The starting trumpet is blown amid great excitement, ushering in an all-singing, all-dancing, regal extravaganza!

'It's certainly original,' said Gavin, feeling that he'd read as much as courtesy could reasonably demand. 'Good luck with it.'

'Not so fast.' Neil took the sheet of paper from him and returned it to the folder. 'This is only a script.'

'What do you mean?'

'It needs music and lyrics,' explained Vincent, 'and that's your department.'

~

'They're pinning their hopes on a musical,' he told Jonathan. 'They reckon that by working to the strengths of individual students, they can produce a hit show, and they want me to write the music and lyrics.'

Jonathan smiled. 'It should be right up your Tin Pan Alley.'

'You might have warned me.'

'And spoil the surprise?'

'Jonathan, it may be a great big joke as far as you're concerned, but when I last wrote song lyrics I was working in a comprehensive school.'

'I know. It's in your CV.'

'Hell's bells, Jonathan, there's a wealth of difference between a school production and the kind of thing these people want.'

'Yes, you'll have to bear that in mind when you start work on it.'

Gavin summoned his patience with an effort. 'But why me?'

'Because composition is your responsibility, because you have experience of musical theatre and because....'

'Yes?'

Jonathan gave a half-shrug, as if the answer were obvious. 'Because no one else is prepared to take it on.'

'And supposing I don't want to either?'

With a calmness that was unsettling, Jonathan said, 'There is an alternative.'

~

Vincent pulled the coffee table to one side to create leg room for Leah, who took the seat gratefully, keeping her injured leg straight.

'Thank you, Vincent. That was very thoughtful of you.'

He lifted the coffee pot and saw her smile. 'What's amusing you?'

'You are. You're so delightfully civilised.'

'Personal standards are vital for morale, and we know how the Inspectorate feel about that.'

'But they were talking about the Music School.'

'Exactly. They take their tea and coffee in chipped and stained pottery mugs.'

'You don't surprise me.' She took the cup of coffee he offered her. Have you met the new music man yet? I forget his name.'

'Gavin? Yes, you missed him by less than half-an-hour.'

'Go on,' she said mischievously, 'spill the beans. What's he like? All wind and organ pipes?'

'No, he's not at all like Jonathan. For one thing, he's much more open-minded, although I have to say he didn't seem terribly keen on the musical.'

'Oh, great.'

'Of course, the problem may have been Neil.'

'You do surprise me.'

Vincent waved an admonishing finger. 'Be fair, Leah. Love him or loathe him, Neil gets results, and he's written a very promising play.'

'Incredibly, but we're still left with a problem.'

'Fear not.' He poured coffee for himself while she waited patiently for him to continue. 'Gavin is going to take the job on in spite of everything.'

'That was a quick U-turn, wasn't it?'

'Yes, but he's not what you'd call a willing convert, at least, not yet.'

'Oh, dear. What a rollercoaster we're riding. Do cut to the punch line, Vincent.'

'All right. Jonathan gave him an ultimatum. It was either the musical or the Popular Music Option.'

She winced. 'How medieval: compliance or The Tower.'

'Hardly that.'

'All right. The musical or the three-minute single. I feel sorry for the poor man already, and I haven't even met him.'

'You shall very soon. I'm calling a meeting for Friday morning. Have you got your diary handy?'

3

Being habitually punctual, Gavin arrived at Vincent's office at five minutes to ten and found Clare alone in her office.

'Hello, Gavin,' she said, turning to greet him. 'How are you coping?'

'I'm... let's say I'm coping.'

'It must be quite a shock, coming here.'

'I don't know,' he said. 'In some respects, it's no different from the last place I was at.'

'How's that?' She seemed genuinely interested.

'How can I describe it? What's a collective name for a lot of egos?'

She looked thoughtful. 'How about a self-obsession?'

'Well done, Clare. Yes, a self-obsession of egos.'

She smiled in sympathy. 'I can't really speak for the Music School,' she said, 'but egocentrics are bound to crop up where you get performers. The trouble is that some of them don't know when to stop performing.'

'That's very true.'

'Vincent's genuine enough. He's a good boss, too.'

'I can see that.'

'Leah's lovely. You know exactly where you are with her.'

'That's encouraging.' After Neil's biased description, he'd been wondering.

'You've met Neil, haven't you?' There was a hint of mischief in her tone.

Gavin nodded grimly.

'You'll need to be firm with him. He's okay, really, when he stops posing.'

'I'll look forward to that.'

She looked at her watch. 'He's always the last to arrive,' she said.

'Maybe he spends too long in front of the mirror.'

She laughed. 'There's someone here who can tell you.'

Gavin turned to see where Clare was looking, and saw a young woman with mid-brown hair caught in a clasp, and friendly, blue eyes. She wore jeans and a floral print blouse, and supported herself with some difficulty on forearm crutches, the difficulty arising from the fact that one hand was also clutching a briefcase.

'Good morning, Clare,' she said.

'Good morning, Leah. Come and meet Gavin from the other side.'

'Hello, Gavin.' Leah removed her right hand from its crutch to shake his. She seemed amused. 'I've always wanted to meet someone from the other side,' she said. It seemed an odd thing to say, considering Neil's warning, but he naturally kept that to himself.

'Hello, Leah. Can I get you a chair?'

'No, thank you all the same. I'll be okay 'til Vincent arrives.'

'Go inside and wait for him there,' suggested Clare.

'No need. He's here now. Good morning, Vincent.'

'Good morning, Leah, Clare and Gavin. I'm sorry I've kept you waiting. Let's go inside.'

Clare asked, 'Coffee, Vincent?'

'Is coffee all right, Gavin?'

'Perfectly.'

'I know you'll have coffee, Leah. Yes please, Clare.' He led the way into his office.

Seeing Leah struggle to move the coffee table, Gavin lifted it aside for her. He asked, 'Is that all right?'

'Lovely, thank you, Gavin.'

'I'm sorry,' said Vincent. 'Gavin beat me to it.'

'Suddenly, there's an embarrassment of gentlemen.' The thought evidently pleased her. 'I suppose,' she said, 'we'll have to be patient and wait for Neil. He wrote the bloody play, after all.'

'I gather he has a reputation for unpunctuality,' said Gavin.

'That's putting it mildly.' Leah placed her crutches beside her chair. 'He'll be late for his own funeral, which may take place sooner than he expects if he goes on being a pain in the neck.'

'As you can see, Gavin,' said Vincent, 'we're one happy family.' He opened the door to admit Clare, who put the tray of coffee things on the table. She had only just left, when someone beat an elaborate tattoo on the door, causing Leah to sigh, and Vincent to say, 'Come in, Neil.'

Neil made his entrance. 'Good morning, souls. You'll never guess what I saw on the way in this morning.'

'Neil,' said Vincent, 'we've been waiting for you so that we can start the meeting.'

Neil's bonhomie gave way to a theatrical sulk. 'Something tells me,' he said, 'that I'm not the flavour of the month.'

Leah gave him a weary look.

Vincent ignored his remark. 'Now you've had time to look at the script, Gavin, have you formed an idea of how you see the music and lyrics evolving?'

'Yes, I have. As I read the plot, the characters have a grandstand view of events on Earth, and each must have his or her feelings and ideas about them. Over hundreds of years, they will have seen musical styles come and go, and they probably have their favourites. I suggest we use a variety of idioms that will showcase our versatility as well as bringing added contrast and irony to the whole production.'

'Not just a pretty face,' observed Neil, clearly impressed by Gavin's reasoning.

Leah appeared thoughtful. She asked, 'Can you give us an example of the kind of irony you mean, Gavin?'

'Yes, I'm talking about pairing characters with the most inappropriate musical idioms. For example, King Philip the Second of Spain might have become enchanted with the Charleston to the extent that he practises it whenever he can. Likewise, King Henry the Seventh, who is always remembered as a dour, no-nonsense kind of monarch, might have taken up tap dancing and be totally bewitched by the Astaire and Rogers era. Naturally, I'll need to discuss each case with you, but that's generally what I have in mind.'

'Are you suggesting,' asked Vincent, 'that we use existing songs?'

'Not for one minute, Vincent. I'm suggesting that I write the songs we need, but in the requisite styles.'

'Are you trying to tell us you can do that?' Even without Neil's theatrical delivery, it would have sounded like a challenge.

'Yes. I have my blind spots, of course. I'm the first to admit that I'm a broken reed when it comes to sixth century Armenian wedding music but, generally speaking, I muddle through.' He thought it was a reasonably polite answer to a particularly impertinent question.

Neil shrugged off the reproach and said, 'Like I said, Gavin, love, you're full of surprises.'

'Just "Gavin", if you don't mind, Neil.' He saw Leah bite her lip, and decided, for the time being, to do the same.

'I'm only extending the hand of friendship.'

'Thank you, Gavin,' said Vincent. 'We'll look forward to hearing your music in due course.'

After the meeting, Leah met Gavin outside.

'You must think I'm an awful bitch,' she said. 'I'm not, really.'

'I'm sure you're not. I find Neil irritating as well. I must have it out with him sooner or later.'

'Well, good luck.' As she turned to go, she dropped her briefcase. 'Oh, hell,' she said.

'Stay there. I'll get it.' He picked it up. 'Let me carry it for you. Where's your office?'

'Just here.' She inclined her head towards the other side of the foyer. 'I'm sure you have things to do, but are you in a hurry?'

He had to report back to Jonathan, but that could wait. He asked, 'What do you have in mind?'

'Just a quick chat about what we've been discussing, but without irritating interruptions.'

'All right.' He followed her to her office, opening the door for her to negotiate the entrance, hindered as she was by her crutches.

'Thank you, Gavin. Would you like coffee, or are you awash with it?'

'Yes, please. I've done more talking than drinking this morning.'

'I know, but it was necessary.'

While she was busy with the coffee, Gavin looked around the walls, which were hung liberally with pictures of, presumably, Leah's ballet idols. He recognised Margot Fonteyn immediately, and then

Natalia Makarova, but he had to read the names of the others: Galina Ulanova, Anna Pavlova and Gelsey Kirkland. There were photographs also of Nijinski, Nureyev, Baryshnikov and Anthony Dowell.

Leah interrupted his scrutiny by asking, 'Are you admiring my rogues' gallery?'

'Yes. I've done the same thing in the past, and I'll probably do it again when I've had time to settle in.'

'Who are your favourites?'

He had to think, as he always did when someone asked him that question. 'Rachmaninov, Chopin, Liszt, Mozart, Irving Berlin, Jerome Kern, Cole Porter, Fred Astaire—'

'Snap.' She pointed to a photograph of Fred Astaire above the coffee machine. 'You have excellent taste, Gavin. How did you become interested in Kern, Porter and Co?'

'My clarinet and sax teacher at school, a chap called Jack Hutchins, was a whale on the music of the 'thirties. He played with some of the West End bands before the war, and he brought me up on a diet of the great songwriters. One of his favourites that he introduced me to was Ray Noble.'

'Yes, he wrote some wonderful stuff.' She was smiling, as if the realisation that they shared a passion for the style and period gave her a special kind of pleasure. 'Where did you go to school?'

'Cullington Comprehensive.'

'I didn't know the West Riding had any comprehensive schools.'

'It became a comprehensive after I started there,' he explained. 'I believe it was a sort of experiment.'

'And a successful one, it seems.'

'Why do you say that?'

She shrugged, as if the answer were obvious. 'It produced a talented musician.'

'You're too kind, but I wasn't the only one. There was another lad there, called Frank Morrison. He's written a lot of commercial stuff, but he's just getting his foot in the TV theme music door. We both went on from school to the College, so we keep in touch.'

'The College?'

'Sorry. The Royal College of Music.' It wasn't what they'd come to discuss, but he had to ask, 'Where did you study?'

'I suppose you could say, the Cory School of Dance, but that's not the whole story.'

Sensing that he'd entered a sensitive area, he waited for her to explain.

'I entered the Royal Ballet School when I was eleven, and I was in my element for a few years, but one day, I was doing some early Christmas shopping in Regent Street, when a car hit me. I was in hospital for months on end; they performed wonders on my various injuries, but I was left with the chronic problem of this damned knee.'

'I'm sorry, Leah. How old were you at the time of the accident?'

'Sixteen.'

'That's horrible.'

'Yes, it shattered my dream as well as my knee.' She poured coffee for them both and said, 'Anyway, I really invited you over to ask how you came to be able to write in so many styles, but I think you've answered that question.'

'Yes, the 'thirties dance music is second nature, but everything else is down, I think, to aural training.'

'I'm still impressed.'

'Well, it's always easier to imitate than it is to be original.'

She nodded. 'I suppose so.'

'Anyway,' he said, conscious that he was there for a purpose, 'we'd better decide how we're going to organise the music for the dance numbers. Once we've decided on the style of dance for each of them, I'll record the music as soon as I can and let you have it.'

'Or you could let me have a copy of the score, and I'll play it for myself.'

He realised he was staring at her.

'What's the matter?' She was clearly amused. 'Have you never met a dancer who could read dots?'

'If I'm honest, no, I haven't.'

'I'm not brilliant,' she admitted, 'but I can fumble through most things.' Still smiling at his confusion, she explained. 'My dad started me on the piano when I was about six. I'd grown up with music around me, so it seemed the natural thing to do. Then, when I was older and living at home after the accident, I used to accompany his rehearsals. He used to write and direct musicals.'

'Professionally?'

'No, he's an amateur, but a gifted one.' She smiled again impishly and said, 'He has a dance band as well.'

Gavin blinked. 'My eyes are being opened today,' he said.

'Oh yes, he does silver weddings and that kind of thing. When the old-timers of Wensleydale want to let their hair down, they send for Freddy Hinchcliffe and the Dalesmen.'

Gavin could find nothing to say.

'I'll let you know when the band gets a local gig, and you can come and hear it.'

4

One week and another physio session later, Leah walked down to the carpark. She had discarded the crutches for the relative freedom of a walking stick, and she was looking forward to spending the weekend at her parents' home in Wensleydale.

She peered across the carpark for her mother's Mini, but without success, so she made herself as comfortable as she could on the low wall that separated the carpark from what the students were now calling the 'campus'. Rain threatened, but it had so far failed to materialise.

She opened her sports bag and took out *If Only They Could Talk* by James Herriot, or Alf Wight, as she knew him. It was a strange feeling, reading a book by someone she'd met, and she was enjoying his descriptions of her native Wensleydale and those Dales farmers, who had changed very little in the thirty-odd years since his arrival from Glasgow. The book was extremely well written, and she was aware of nothing else until a man's voice broke her concentration.

'My dear old thing, harm can come to a girl, sitting on a cold, stone wall.'

She looked up and saw a tall, grey-haired, immaculately-dressed man of middle years.

'Bailey!' She tried to stand up.

'Let me help you.' He supported her until she was on her feet, and then picked up her sports bag.

She inclined her cheek to accept a kiss from her godfather, and said, 'It's great to see you again, Bailey, but where's Mum?'

'She couldn't make it, old thing. She's so busy, she asked me to come instead.' Seeing her pick up her stick with her right hand, he offered her his arm, which she took with her other hand.

'What's happened to make my mum too busy to come for me?'

'I'll explain as we go, Leah.'

He was his usual unfazed self, so she presumed that nothing terrible could have befallen her mother, and she contained herself until they reached Bailey's Rover.

'I've pushed the seat back to give you more room,' he said, opening the passenger door for her. 'How's it coming along, by the way?'

'It's improving. At least, I'm rid of the crutches.'

'I thought you were the epitome of grace and poise on those crutches.'

'You're priceless, Bailey.' She settled comfortably into her seat and said, 'Don't keep me in suspense. What's happened to Mum?'

'Your dear parent is in the very pinnacle of health, Leah. She's simply looking after Martin, who's been involved in an accident.'

'Martin?' It hadn't occurred to her that her brother might be the problem. As far as she knew, he wasn't expected home.

'He's not hurt,' Bailey assured her, 'not even walking wounded, but he's shaken.'

'What happened?'

Bailey turned on to the A61 before answering. 'He was driving through Leeds,' he told her, 'when an elderly soul tried to cross Boar Lane without looking. A chap on a motorbike was coming the other way and he swerved to miss her. In doing so, he lost his balance, or whatever the technical jargon is, and fell in front of Martin's car.'

'So it wasn't Martin's fault?'

'Not in any way, shape or form. Absolutely not guilty and free to leave the court with an unblemished character. The boys in blue are quite categorical about that.'

'Thank goodness for that.' It was a lot to take in. Somewhat guiltily, she asked, 'How's the motorcyclist?'

'He didn't make it, I'm afraid. That's why Martin's so shaken.' He pointed to the passenger glove compartment and said, 'There are some wine gums in there, by the way.'

'I'm not surprised.' She added, 'I mean, that he's shaken, poor lad. The wine gums are a total surprise, but quite typical of you, Bailey.'

'That's what godfathers are for, or so it says in all the books I've read on the subject.'

She laughed. 'I don't believe you've read anything of the sort. You've simply made it up as you've gone along.'

'All right. We can't all be scholars. How goes it at the venerable pile, by the way?'

'We're trying to organise the musical I told you about. It's actually a very good play, but the chap who wrote it is impossible.' She tore open the bag and asked, 'Would you like a wine gum, Bailey?'

'No, thank you all the same. I've had too many already.' He pulled out to pass a dawdling Austin Maxi. 'What do you mean about the writer chappie being impossible?'

'How can I describe him? I've accused you of being a poser, but Neil's a lost cause.'

Bailey feigned shock. 'Me, a *poseur*? The very idea.'

'You're full of shit, Bailey. You know you are.' The fun in her eyes belied any real censure.

'Oh well, if I'm not as bad as this character.... What did you say his name is?'

'Neil, and you're nothing like as bad as he is.'

'Not a hopeless case, then?' Bailey's expression took on a hint of optimism.

'Of course you're not, and I wouldn't have you any other way.'

'Good, because I'm too old to change.'

Remembering her manners, Leah asked, 'How are Elaine and Janice?'

'Elaine is flourishing, and as sensible as ever. How she puts up with me I just don't know.'

'Neither does anyone else.'

'You're maligning me again, Leah, but I'll turn the other cheek and tell you that Janice is cock-a-hoop about her new job at the dairy.'

'What job is that?' It was news to Leah.

'She takes tea and coffee on a trolley to everyone in the office and spends the rest of her time working the bottle-washing machine. She says everyone is always pleased to see her.'

'Of course they are. A cup of tea is always welcome, and it's difficult not to like her.' Janice was the only daughter of Bailey and Elaine. She was a year younger than Leah, but she was reckoned to have a mental age of eight.

'Tell me about this Neil merchant.'

'Okay.' She wondered how best to describe him, and decided to begin in general terms. 'There's a popular theatrical stereotype,' she said, 'who addresses his fellow male thespians as "love", "sweetie" and "darling" without necessarily being gay. Are you with me so far?'

'I think so.' Bailey's tone implied otherwise. 'Is this normally a light-hearted greeting between theatricals?'

'No, Bailey. The word "gay" is used nowadays to mean homosexual.'

'My dear child, are you quite serious?'

'It's the accepted term,' she assured him.

'But why can't they just call them homos or quee—?'

'Because gay people find those names offensive, and now it's legal, we have to try not to give offence.'

'And to think I used to describe myself as a gay bachelor.' Bailey seemed to be in shock.

'In those days, Bailey, no one would have given it a second thought, especially in Wensleydale, or any Dale, for that matter. Now, may I continue?'

'Please do, but with some regard for my sensibilities, if you don't mind. I mean, shock can do things to a chap of my years.'

'You'll survive. Anyway, Neil is very much of that stereotype, and it doesn't end there.'

'I'm beginning to wish I hadn't asked.' He adjusted an air vent on the facia so that it directed a stream of cool air towards him. At the same time, the first spots of rain appeared on the windscreen, so he switched on the wipers.

'Basically,' said Leah, 'he's as camp as a two-man tent.'

'He's what?'

'Oh, Bailey, don't tell me you don't know what "camp" means.'

'I spent most of the war in one, dearest goddaughter of mine, but I suspect you're referring to one of a different and possibly esoteric kind.'

'Almost. Someone who is *camp* is artificially effeminate.'

'How odd. So he minces around, calling men "darling" even though he's not....'

'Gay. You've got the idea, Bailey, more or less.' She wondered, not for the first time, how people of her parents' generation could be so obtuse. She decided to press on nevertheless. 'Irritating though he is,' she said, 'that's not the worst of it. I worry, sometimes, about the effect he has on some of the students. Some of them are impressionable and vulnerable.'

'I think if I were one of them, and he called me "darling", I'd be less than impressed. I'd probably react, you know.'

'I'm sure of it.' Leah thought of Bailey's reputation as a light-heavyweight boxer, but it was impossible to imagine him as a drama student, anyway.

⁓⁓

Having joined her mum in thanking Bailey for his kindness, she waved him off before going indoors to greet her brother.

'Martin,' she said, giving him a hug, 'what a lousy thing to happen. Bailey told me all about it, so you've no need. Come and sit down.'

They sat together on the sofa, siblings but very different. Where Leah had inherited her mother's brown hair and light complexion, Martin was as dark-haired as his father had been before turning prematurely grey. He was also a great deal less out-going than his sister, even when circumstances were normal; in fact, he seemed at times withdrawn.

'Tea, everyone,' announced their mother, placing her tray on the coffee table. 'Martin's in the front bedroom, Leah, so you have the little one.'

'That's all right, Mum. I don't take up much room.'

'I don't have to have the big room,' said Martin generously.

'Yes, you do,' Leah told him. 'You're so untidy, you need room to spread everything out.'

'You were both untidy as teenagers,' her mum reminded her, 'but it's still nice to have you home, if only for the weekend.'

Martin's eye fell on Leah's outstretched leg. He asked, 'How's the knee?'

'On the mend, thank you. I'm going to need it before long, with the show we're putting on.'

Her mother asked, 'What style of dance does it call for?'

'You name it, Mum. There'll be ballet, jazz and tap, at least. The new music lecturer wants to make it an assortment of musical styles.'

What her mother thought about that remained a mystery, because she was distracted by something scratching at the outer kitchen door. 'Oh,' she said, 'I'd forgotten she was in the garden.' She hurried into the kitchen to open the door.

She returned with an Aberdeen Terrier, whose wagging tail told Leah and Martin that she was delighted to see them, even though they were complete strangers.

'Hello,' said Leah, leaning forward to stroke her. 'Who are you?'

'This is Rhea,' announced her mother. 'We only got her last Friday. She's two years old, and her previous owner died quite suddenly.'

'She's lovely,' said Martin, 'but she's going to be confused when she hears you say, "Leah".'

Rhea proved his point by giving him her full attention.

'Ah, but she lives here,' said Leah. 'I only come visiting.'

'It's a funny sort of name. How do you spell it?'

'Of course,' said Leah, 'all your letters are numbers, aren't they?'

'I've seen two spellings,' said their mother, 'but hers is spelt R-h-e-a.'

'It's still a funny name,' Martin insisted.

'Rhea was a Greek goddess,' she told them.

'Was she? I'd never have known that.'

'We had one called Thea,' said his mum. 'Leah might remember her, but you won't, Martin. She was a rescued dog, like Rhea.'

Suddenly, the name triggered a memory for Leah. 'Wasn't she the one that stopped a cricket match? I remember hearing about it.'

'That's right. Your dad was very embarrassed.'

Martin asked, 'What happened?'

'She chased after the ball and then stood guard over it, so the whole thing stopped until your dad retrieved the ball, and I took Thea back to the pavilion. Otherwise, it was a good day for your dad in terms of wickets and runs.'

'I can't imagine the Old Man playing cricket,' said Martin.

His mother gave him a stern look. 'He wouldn't be very pleased if he heard you calling him that.'

'You could always put it to the test,' suggested Leah, nodding towards the window, where her father's car was now visible.

Rhea was already at the door, waiting with suppressed excitement until the door opened and the rapturous welcome commenced.

'Hello, Rhea,' said her master. 'I'm sorry I couldn't take you this afternoon. I had to photograph a border collie of uncertain disposition.'

'I thought that was a general breed description,' said Leah.

'I was being generous to the breed. Ah, thank you, SP.' He accepted a cup of tea, which he set down on the coffee table while he kissed his wife. 'Leah,' he said, 'have you got a kiss for the Old Man?'

Leah kissed her father, and Martin shifted guiltily as he shook his hand.

'Come and sit with us, Dad,' said Leah.

'Between you two? No fear,' he said, taking the other armchair. 'I don't want to be caught in the cross-fire.'

'Mum's been telling us about the time Thea stopped the cricket match,' said Leah.

'Oh, that was a long time ago. I think it was before either of you were born.'

Martin was still struggling with names. 'He asked, 'Was Thea a Greek goddess too?'

'Yes, she was,' said Leah. 'She was one of the Titans. I suppose it's a coincidence that Rhea's name comes from the same place?'

Her mother nodded.

'What I can't understand,' said Martin, 'is why anyone can be bothered to read about Greek mythology or, for that matter, anything else that's not true.'

Leah's eyes grew wide, and she said, 'We have a philistine among us.' Then, with a generous smile, she turned to him and said, 'Never mind, Martin. You're *our* philistine, and that's what matters.'

Whatever their cultural differences, Leah and Martin went to the Shearer's Arms after dinner, leaving their parents to talk.

'I imagine a drink will do him good, SP.'

'Something needs to. He's all right, sitting and talking with us. It's when he's alone that he thinks about it and gets into a state.'

Freddy lifted the bottle of wine but, seeing Sylvia shake her head, refilled his glass instead. 'Has he seen a doctor?'

'No. David stopped by this afternoon, on his way to a patient, and he suggested it, but Martin won't hear of it.'

Freddy remembered Sylvia's brother-in-law giving him the same advice thirty years earlier, when he returned from Poland and Germany. 'It's a shame he's not at all interested in fishing,' he said.

'Oh, Freddy, it's not bound to work for everyone. Fishing at Redmire Falls did the trick for my dad after the first war, and it did the same for you, but you're expecting a lot if you think it'll cure Martin's state of mind.'

'If he'd talk to me about it, it would be a start.' He reflected briefly and said, 'I'd be surprised if he talked to me about anything. I think he sees me as a stranger on the planet.'

'I'm sure you're not the only father with that problem.'

'Probably not, SP, but that doesn't make me feel any better about it.'

Thoughtfully, Sylvia poured herself another glass of wine. 'There's a world beyond fly fishing,' she said.

'I'm well aware of that.'

'No, Freddy, hear me out. Have you thought of talking to Martin about something that interests him?'

'Electronics? Computers? Software, whatever that is? They really do exist on an alien planet.'

'He's interested in more than those things. What about those expensive binoculars you got for him last Christmas?'

5

Freddy was surprised, that Sunday, when Martin agreed to go with him to Redmire Falls. He was also pleased to see the Ross binoculars hanging from his son's neck.

It was a poignant journey, and not just because of Martin's current preoccupation. Freddy had been used to fishing with Sylvia's father; in fact, Walter had introduced him both to fly fishing and to Redmire itself on the day after VE Day. They had gone on, after that, to fish together as close friends for thirty years, almost until Walter's death in May.

Saddened though he was, Freddy was now taking the next generation down to the Falls, and with yet another companion. Rhea lay on the back seat with no idea of her destination, but happy enough to be in her new owner's company. She had also formed a new friendship, with Martin.

Freddy parked at Mill Farm, where they unloaded the fishing gear and set off down the lane, with Rhea busily sniffing the gorse that grew in profusion beside the track.

Presently, they came to Cherry Tree Wood, which had been a favourite haunt for Walter and Freddy for so long, and there they unfolded their seats.

Martin had been quiet on the way down from Redmire, so it was a surprise when he said suddenly, 'Sparrowhawk.' Lifting his binoculars, he tracked it across the treescape on the opposite bank. 'Here, Dad,' he said, handing his binoculars to Freddy and pointing excitedly. 'Orange breast and blue-grey wings. Can you see it?'

'Yes, I've got it.'

'You can hear the little birds raising the alarm.'

'Yes, I can.' Freddy had never taken much notice of birdsong, except as an accompaniment to an agreeable landscape, but he could hear those little birds now, spreading the word that mortal danger was near.

It was as if Martin had woken from a long sleep, because he was suddenly animated, sighting and identifying birds with a sureness that astonished Freddy.

After a while, Martin said conversationally, 'Good bins, these.'

'Make the most of them, Martin. You won't get any more where they came from.'

Martin looked surprised. 'Have they stopped trading?'

'Yes, earlier his year.'

'Why? Did they just go broke?'

'Yes, the competition from Germany and Japan was too much for them.' He reflected on the misfortune. 'You know,' he said, 'I carried a pair of Ross night glasses all the time I was airborne.'

'Did the Navy use anything else?'

'No, only Ross.'

'That was quite an endorsement, wasn't it?'

It occurred to Freddy that it was possibly the longest conversation he'd had with his son in a long time. He wondered how to prolong it, and decided eventually to take Walter's example.

'I expect you know why I asked you to come today.'

Martin nodded. 'Mum told me.'

'You see, I know what it's like to close my eyes and see the horrors I thought I'd left behind me.'

Martin glanced at him in mute surprise before looking down again and saying, 'I can see that poor lad in the road, the blood and everything. He was only seventeen.' He was quiet, and then he said, 'I'll have to go to a coroner's inquest.' Rhea was licking his hand in what might have been sympathy, but then something distracted her, and she went off in search of new scents.

'Don't worry about that, Martin. I'll go with you.'

With another look of surprise, he asked, 'What about work?'

'The inquest is more important than work. At least, your... situation is.'

'Thanks, Dad.' He continued to stare at the ground. Eventually, he asked, 'What did you mean?'

31

'About what?'

'When you said you knew what it was like.'

Freddy wondered how to begin. He'd never found it easy to confide, and he suspected his son was experiencing the same awkwardness. He braced himself and said, 'When I came home from Poland and Germany, I had to make a huge adjustment. I'd come from a place of hunger, toil, Nazi brutality and the coldest winter on record, to the beauty of Wensleydale and the warm hospitality of your granddad and grandma. Your mum was still in Malta. It was a colossal adjustment, as I said, and I was struggling with it.' Thirty years had passed, and the memory of the emotional conflict was as stark as ever. 'I'd seen men treated worse than cattle, I'd seen cold-blooded murder, and I thought it was all behind me until I came to Leyburn, where your grandparents lived in those days. That's when the nightmares and daytime horrors began.'

He stopped, unsure whether Martin was listening or simply locked in his own awful episode, and then his son looked up as if inviting him to continue.

'The day after VE Day, your grandad brought me down here and told me about his state of mind when he returned from France with a shattered knee and horrors that followed him home and refused to leave him. I wish to goodness he was here now, Martin, because he described things much better than I can. He gave me some advice, you see, that changed everything for me. He said, every time I was visited by the memory of the salt mine, I should think immediately of the good things I saw around me, here, at Redmire Falls: the river, the trees, the fish in the water, and the tranquillity of the place.'

Martin was looking at him now with fresh concentration that encouraged him to go on.

'It was good advice, Martin, and it worked. He mentioned a song made popular at the time by Bing Crosby: "Accentuate the Positive, Eliminate the Negative", and that's what you must do. Let the good drive out the bad. It worked for him, it worked for me, and I think it could do the same for you.'

Freddy had found it as difficult as ever to open up; it was a standing joke between Sylvia and him, that he was a son of Kingston-Upon-Hull, where the baring of souls was as rare as daffodils in

December, and some things never changed. Even so, he felt that he'd achieved something with Martin, and it had been well worth the discomfort.

Back home, Martin went upstairs to change, and Sylvia took the opportunity to ask, 'How did it go?'

'I didn't catch a single trout.'

She gave him a grown-up look. 'Oh, Freddy, you know what I mean.'

'We watched some birds and we did a lot of talking; at least, I did.'

'Do you think it did some good?'

'I'm sure it did, SP.'

'Redmire Falls are still working their magic, then?' Her eyes were wet.

'Of course, and I think your dad would have been pleased.'

❦

'Do you think Martin will be all right, Mum?'

It was Monday morning, and Sylvia was driving Leah back to the college.

'I think so. Your dad had a long talk with him yesterday, and he knows we're all behind him.'

'He isolates himself from us, you know.'

'Oh, Leah, that's a bit strong.'

'I'm not being critical, Mum. I'm as concerned about him as you are. I just mean that he assumes he's apart from the rest of us. I think it's because you, Dad and I are all so arty and expressive, and he's.... I suppose he's left-brained. He must feel that he's the odd one out.'

'What on earth does "left-brained" mean?'

Leah waited for her mother to overtake a haycart and tractor, and explained. 'They say that aesthetic activity takes place in the right side of the brain, and the left side deals basically with logic, maths and that kind of thing. Working as readily as he does with computers, Martin is obviously a logical thinker. Do you remember how good he was at maths?'

'Yes, I do.'

'It was just as well, because if he'd struggled, none of us could have helped him.'

'No.' Sylvia peered at her fuel gauge and said, 'I must fill up with petrol after I drop you.' She returned her attention to Leah. 'Yes, that's true, Leah. It was English that Martin always found difficult.'

'Well, there you are. I was only joking on Friday, when I said all his letters were numbers, but it's basically true.'

'At all events,' said her mother, 'spending the day with your dad did him a lot of good.' The thought seemed to lead to another, because she asked, 'Did you know he was keen on birds?'

'Yes, he's been into it for some time.'

Her mother winced. 'What a peculiar turn of phrase. Wherever did "into it" come from?'

'I don't know. I must have picked it up from the students.'

'Anyway, how did you find that out? We'd no idea.'

'I asked him what he'd got those binoculars for, and he went quiet, the way he does, so I teased him a bit. It was just before he moved out, and I asked him if he'd got them to peep at Wendy Albright across the road. You know how she never bothers to close her curtains, and I'm sure Martin's seen all she's got to offer.' She glanced sideways at her mother, expecting a reaction. 'Of course, he denied it. That's when he told me they were for birdwatching, the feathered kind, that is.'

'Leah, that was an awful thing to say to him. You know he takes everything seriously.'

'It's funny that he never plucked up the courage to ask her out. I must get on to him about that.'

'Don't you dare.'

'He could get to know her better, what she looks like with her clothes on, for instance.' She grinned impishly. 'At least for a while.'

Her mother glanced at her, no doubt taking in her teasing smile. 'Leah, behave yourself. I despair of your generation, I really do.' Possibly in an effort to restore the conversation to an acceptable level of decency, she said, 'Wendy's in the pantomime. She's got the part of Dick Whittington.'

'What pantomime?'

'Yoredale Players. Your dad's written it and cast it, and I'm in charge of dance, as usual. Rehearsals have already begun.'

'He never said anything about it to me.'

'Well,' said her mother dryly, 'we did have a distraction this weekend.'

'Of course.' Leah considered the information so far and said, 'Wendy's a good choice. She has the equipment for it.'

'What do you mean?'

'Her legs. She'll look great in fishnets.' She smiled mischievously. 'Martin will blow a fuse when he sees her on stage.'

'Oh, Leah.'

'Mind you, he's already seen more of her than the audience ever will.'

'Leah, you're the limit.'

Gavin had no idea how the giants of musical comedy worked, but his method was to write the music first, and then the lyrics. With a theme running through his head, he was able to visualise the characters on stage and get a feel for the whole experience. It gave him ideas for lyrics that might not normally have come to him.

The show was to begin with the monarchs on stage, complaining in turn about their inability to join the heroes, heroines and great achievers in the Upper Chambers. Their snatches of dialogue were to be spoken in rhythm to musical accompaniment, which would be easy enough. This would be interrupted by a trumpet fanfare, and the voice of the Celestial Messenger would announce the vacancy. Gavin imagined four majestic chords from the orchestra leading into the opening chorus.

He saw the competition not so much as an election, but a race. That would make it more exciting. He visualised a crowd behind the railings at a race meeting, and a rhythmical accompaniment evoking the sound of horses' hoofbeats came to him. Next came the first eight bars, repeated, and then the middle eight. Confident that his idea would work, he put pencil to paper.

He'd almost sketched the first eight bars, when there was a knock on the door and Neil walked in.

'Good morning, Gavin love.'

'Good morning, Neil, and just "Gavin" will do, as I believe I've already told you.'

'I just bobbed in to ask how you're getting on.'

'I'm sketching the opening chorus.'

'At your desk?'

Gavin sighed. 'Should I be using someone else's?'

Neil gave him a look of reproach. 'Someone got out of bed on the wrong side this morning, I can tell. I simply expected you to write music at the piano.'

'I'm sorry to disappoint you, Neil, but I always work this way. I may occasionally try out an idea on the piano, but I prefer, generally speaking, to work at my desk.' He wished he would simply go away.

'In that case, how do you know what the music is going to sound like?'

Gavin was about to tell him, but decided against it. Instead, he said, 'I don't. It always comes as a great big surprise.'

Neil made no response. Instead, he asked, 'Have you been to Leah's office yet?' The question came with a hint of mischief.

'Yes, but not this morning.'

'You'll have seen the photos of her girlfriends, then?'

'Neil, I'm busy. Is there a purpose to this visit, or would you be better employed elsewhere? I ask the question as someone who simply wishes to work undisturbed.'

'Oh, we *are* in a mood. I shall go.' He opened the door with a flourish.

'Goodbye, Neil.'

'Goodbye, Gavin love.'

It seemed to Gavin that the showdown must occur soon. Unfortunately, at least for the time being, he was too busy.

6

The first morning of the new term had been devoted to a general introduction by Jonathan Best, followed by the allocation of group and individual timetables. Gavin's first session with the External Diploma class came after lunch. The subject was Analysis.

'Can anyone tell me the meaning of "form"?' It was difficult question for anyone to answer without prior notice, but it usually started a discussion, which was always a good thing.

One student appeared ready to make his contribution.

'Yes?'

'Gavin, this musical we've been told about—'

'I'll be happy to discuss it later.'

'But it's important.' The student wore a CND badge and an earnest expression.

'So is your ability to analyse an unseen piece of music, which is one of the ultimate aims of this course.'

'Yes, but you're not listening.'

'Neither are you. What's your name?'

'Kevin.'

'All right, Kevin, as I said, I'll be happy to discuss the musical with you later. For now, I want to concentrate on musical analysis, and I shouldn't be surprised if your fellow students are also quite keen to do that.'

'You're not interested, are you?'

'At the right time, Kevin, I am, but this is not the right time. May I continue?'

Kevin turned, presenting his right profile and rested his chin firmly on his hand. Gavin was unable to see his lower lip.

'Would someone like to have a go at defining "form"?'

A student on the front row opened his mouth to speak, and then decided otherwise. Elsewhere, faces were blank, until a girl raised her hand to say, 'Is it shape?'

'Shape is very important,' said Gavin, 'very important indeed, but it's not the whole picture.'

Another student asked, 'Is it the same as a pattern?'

'That's another excellent suggestion. "Pattern" and "shape" are both key words.' He decided to take pity on them. 'Form is basically *structure*. It has shape, as we've heard, and it conforms to a pattern. There's a story about the young Mozart, who used to amuse himself at the dining table by folding napkins into intricate shapes and patterns. He was, of course, one of the outstanding composers of the Classical Period, when form, as some of you might say, "ruled okay".'

There was general laughter, and Kevin resumed a frontal pose.

'Who uses napkins?'

'I beg your pardon, Kevin?'

'Napkins are a trapping of bourgeois society. I asked you, who uses napkins?'

'In this case, Mozart did, although I'm afraid it's a little late to challenge him about the habit, and I should like to continue.'

Kevin reverted to his sulking pose.

'So, Mozart was keenly interested in both shape and pattern, but he knew that they weren't the whole picture. He knew better than any of us that form, or structure, was an amalgam of pattern, shape and sound. The pattern is a basic plan and the themes give it shape, sound makes it into music. So far, so good, but what gives it drama?'

To his relief, a discussion evolved, during which he was able to introduce the concept of conflict, and therefore drama, brought about by keys, with their individual identities and qualities, at odds with one another. It was a useful session and, with ten minutes in hand, he kept his bargain with Kevin.

'Kevin,' he said, 'as I recall, you have something to say about the musical.'

Kevin released a sigh that Gavin interpreted as one of patience finally rewarded. 'I've been trying to say that it's a ridiculous subject for a play. I don't agree with the Queen or any of her family.'

'On what particular subject do you disagree with them?'

'No, you're not listening again.'

'I am listening, Kevin. You said you disagreed with them. Tell me about this disagreement. When did it take place?'

'No, you have to listen. I've never met any of them, and I don't want to. They shouldn't be allowed.'

'Ah, you were trying to say that you're anti-royalist.'

'Yes.' Kevin rolled his eyes upward, like an impatient teacher dealing with an obtuse child.

'That's your right in a free society, Kevin, just as it's the right of those involved to produce a musical based on any premise of their choice, just as long as it doesn't break the law or offend public sensibilities.'

'It offends my sensibilities.'

'But you can't have seen the script, and I've only just written the first music number. How can it offend your sensibilities or any other part of you?'

'Royalty is offensive.'

Some of the students were becoming restless. One said, 'Shut up, Kevin. You're making a fool of yourself.'

'No,' said Gavin, 'let's continue with the argument. You object to it, Kevin, because you feel that this country should be a republic. That is a political stance. On the other hand, the show is a diversion, no more and no less than that. It neither supports nor criticises the monarchy as an institution. It's simply taking a light-hearted look at a group of past monarchs in the most improbable situation imaginable.'

Kevin's patience had reached its limit. 'That's typical of your kind,' he said, standing up to leave. 'You won't take anything seriously.'

When Kevin had gone, slamming the door behind him, Gavin spoke to the class. 'I'm sorry we were distracted at the beginning,' he said. 'If there's anything you want to discuss about today's topic, you know where to find me. It's an ever-open door.'

On her way out, the girl who had asked about shape, said, 'Gavin, you have the patience of a saint.'

Gavin smiled and picked up his notes. As he did so, he saw a scribbled message. It read, *Gavin love, can you make a meeting in my office at 5:15?* It was signed *Neil.* It seemed that his patience was about to be tested again.

He was about to leave the building, when Jonathan hailed him from his office door.

'Gavin, have you a moment?'

'I'm on my way to a meeting, Jonathan.'

'It shouldn't take long,' he said, holding his door open in invitation.

Gavin looked at his watch. He had a little over five minutes to spare. 'All right,' he said.

'How was your first day?'

'Quite good.'

'The thing is, I've had a student to see me, Kevin McNamara. He said you'd been challenging his political convictions this afternoon. He was quite worked up about it.' His attitude was avuncular. 'You know, you mustn't get into political arguments with students. It's not why we're here.'

'I didn't.'

'But he was most insistent that you had.'

'If you're prepared to listen, Jonathan, I'll tell you what happened.'

'Very well.'

'He interrupted a session on form to register his objection to the musical, on the basis that it was about royalty, an institution to which he is strongly opposed. I told him that the musical is nothing more than a harmless diversion, and he refused to accept that. He stormed off, telling me that my sort never take anything seriously. That was all.'

'Well, you'll have to be very careful with him. He's obviously very committed.'

Gavin was heartily sick of Kevin McNamara, but he held his feelings in check. 'He's committed to politics, yes, but I doubt if he learned anything this afternoon about analysis.' He stood up to leave. 'Is that all, Jonathan?'

'Yes, as long as you remember to be careful in future.'

'I was very careful this afternoon. Unlike Kevin McNamara, I was also mindful that the other students deserved some of my attention. If he does it again, I'll suggest he argues with you. At least, then, you'll know what I'm dealing with.'

'Go to your meeting, Gavin.' Jonathan gave the instruction with patronising calmness, so that Gavin thought seriously about carrying out his threat. The outcome might be interesting.

It was his first day at the chalk face and he was already wound up. As he walked across to Drama and Dance, he made a conscious effort to put Kevin and Jonathan out of his thoughts.

He found Leah outside Neil's office, but there was no sign of Neil.

'Hello, Leah.'

'Hello, Gavin. How was your first day?'

'Fine until I had to put a troublesome student in his place. He reported me to Jonathan, would you believe?'

'Already?'

'Incredibly, yes.' He told her about the argument and then about his meeting with Jonathan.

'Good luck with Jonathan,' she said. 'He was over here earlier, loitering with contempt. His attitude towards everything is either contemptuous or patronising.'

'Except Bach and the organ.'

'Oh, Bach gets his vote, does he? Lucky man.'

Gavin looked around inquiringly and said, 'There's no sign of Neil. Do you think he's forgotten about the meeting?'

Leah glanced at her watch. 'No, it's only twenty-past. That's early for him.' To pass the time, she said, 'I told you about my dad writing musicals, didn't I? He's written a pantomime now.'

'Which one?'

'Dick Whittington.'

'I used to love pantomimes when I was a kid. I haven't seen one for, oh... seventeen, maybe eighteen years.'

'You do sound old,' she teased. 'Come and see this one. They're putting it on in January.'

'You know, I think I will.'

'You think you will what?' Neil's voice surprised them both, coming from behind them.

'I was saying,' said Gavin, 'that you seemed to have forgotten about the meeting, so I thought I'd go and do something useful.'

'Oh well, now we're all here we can get started.' He opened his office door and held it for them. 'I was caught by one of the "God Squad" objecting to the play. He said it was blasphemous, although how he knows that at this stage is a mystery.'

'For goodness' sake, Neil,' said Leah, 'if you want them to re-spect what we are doing, the least you can do is to show them some respect by referring to their organisation by its proper name.'

'What is its proper name?'

'It's the Christian Student Fellowship.'

'All right, I'll genuflect next time I see them.'

Leah made no effort to conceal her disapproval. 'That,' she said, 'is just the kind of attitude that will get their backs up.'

Gavin pulled aside the coffee table for Leah. 'I had a similar brush this afternoon, with an ardent republican,' he said.

'Thank you, Gavin.' Leah took her seat and said, 'Having heard the story, I know you dealt with the student in a professional manner.'

Neil appeared to dismiss the subject. 'Now, dears,' he said, 'let's look at the staging for the opening sequence.'

Gavin asked, 'Are you going to call a meeting to discuss each music number? I only ask because it would take up a lot of time.'

'No, love, just for each scene.'

There was a knock, and Vincent entered the office.

'I'm sorry,' he said. 'My meeting went on over long.'

'There was no need to come to this one,' said Neil pointedly.

'It's no trouble. Please carry on.'

Neil looked down at his notebook. 'Right,' he said, 'we've decid-ed that the trumpet call and announcement will be followed by the opening chorus. Tell us about that, Gavin love.'

'Just "Gavin", please, Neil. I suggest we use a race as an analogy for the competition. Don't forget that racing is the sport of kings. There's an insistent hoofbeat rhythm, and I see the characters on stage as racegoers following an invisible race.'

'I've seen the score, Neil,' said Leah. 'It works well and builds up to the perfect climax for an opening number.'

'Perhaps you'd let me in on this, Gavin love,' said Neil, looking affronted. 'I am the director, after all.'

'That's no trouble. Can you read music?'

'Of course not, dear.'

'In that case, I'll send you a tape.'

'Thank you, love.'

There was some discussion about involving dancers in the opening chorus, Leah being in favour of it on the basis that it would add to the excitement and give the audience a taste of things to follow. Neil was lukewarm at first, but she and Gavin persuaded him that the success of the number as a spectacular introduction to the play depended on it.

'Okay,' said Neil, 'has either of you anything to add? Leah darling?'

'No.'

'Gavin love?'

'Neil, I've told you repeatedly to stop calling me those ridiculous names. I've had more than enough of it.'

Neil looked around the gathering with a whimsical smile. ' "The lady doth protest too much, methinks." '

Gavin forced himself to remain calm. 'Look,' he said, 'I have no wish to offend anyone in this room, but I have to say that I'm one hundred percent straight, and I resent being spoken to, Neil, as if I'm the latest object of your fancy.'

'So now you're saying *I'm* gay.'

'Stop, both of you.' Vincent held up his hands. 'This is the reason I insisted on being here. We have to work together on this production, and I really can't see that happening if this state of affairs is going to continue.'

Neil gave an effeminate shrug. 'Tell *him* that.'

'Do grow up, Neil. You've insisted on addressing Gavin in that way, even though he's asked you not to, and now you want to blame him because he objects to it.'

Leah, who had been silent until then, said, 'It's par for the course, Vincent. What do you expect?'

'I expect the team to behave professionally, and not let differences – and I use the word in its broadest sense – impede what we're trying to achieve.' He looked around at everyone, finally settling on Neil, and said, 'First of all, Neil you must stop calling Gavin "love", "darling", "sweetie", or any of those intimate forms of address to which you're so attached. Now, Gavin, if he does that, are you prepared to work with him without friction?'

'Of course.'

'Leah, can I ask you to bury the hatchet as well?'

'I'll make an effort, Vincent.'

'Thank you.'

Vincent and Leah got up to leave, while Gavin sat for a moment in wistful reflection. When he stood up, Neil said, 'I *am* straight, you know.'

'Maybe you're an excellent actor,' Gavin told him, 'because the camp act is very convincing.'

'I'll try to keep it butch from now on,' said Neil.

For the sake of the show, Gavin shook hands with him.

As he left Neil's office, he saw Leah leaving hers. He asked, 'Can I give you a lift anywhere?'

She gave him an odd look and said, 'No, thanks. I've got a taxi coming.'

7

The week improved, so that, by Wednesday morning, Gavin was beginning to remember why he'd chosen to do the work he was doing. His day began with a piano lesson with a new student called Clive, who had been working on the first of Beethoven's piano sonatas.

'It was one of the Grade Eight pieces I didn't choose for the exam,' explained Clive, whose youthful appearance seemed to mask a mature attitude towards his studies.

'What did you play instead?'

'One by Mozart, the B flat, K 545.'

'It was a good choice. Okay, would you like to start?' He sat back to listen.

Clive was playing it well, articulating the *staccato* opening cleanly and bringing out the contrast between the dynamics in the transition into the second group of themes. That was where Gavin had to stop him.

'I'm sorry, Clive. You've made an excellent job of it so far. Let me ask you, though, how this passage is supposed to be articulated.'

Clive looked surprised. Finally, he said, '*Legato*. Is that what you mean?'

'That's exactly what I mean, but what does *legato* mean?'

Clive looked at him again strangely. 'Smoothly,' he said.

'Oh, but it means much more than that. Do you know what a ligature is?'

'Isn't it a thing for tying a reed to a clarinet?'

'That's one kind of ligature. It's basically something that ties things together. It comes from the same root as *legato*, so we have to think in terms of tying together. Each successive note is played as if it's tied to the one before it. Now, let's try that passage again.' It was teaching as it should be, and Gavin enjoyed the lesson as much as Clive said he had.

'Well done, Clive. See you next week.'

'Thanks, Gavin. "Bye.'

After the coffee break, Gavin had a composition session with the External Diploma class he'd met earlier. For the morning's session, he'd broken them up into three groups of three, each receiving a twenty-minute tutorial. His first group comprised two female students and one male. He had to stop thinking in terms of girls and boys. Five years had elapsed since the age of majority was reduced to 18, and most of the students were now technically adults.

He introduced their task for the week. 'I want you to write a piece of incidental music,' he told them. 'You can write it in piano score for now, and maybe score it later for a group of instruments.'

One student raised her hand. He imagined that some habits were hard to break.

'Yes, Theresa?' Happily, most students were wearing name badges until the staff learned their names.

'What's it about?'

'I'm coming to that. It has to be about something or someone creeping up on something or someone else. Think about what can happen during the pursuit. Let's say someone is pursuing a woman. The victim hears something and turns, so that the pursuer has to dodge into a shop doorway. Then, the victim is convinced she's being followed, so she walks faster.' He was gratified by the look of involvement on the students' faces.

'The pursuer responds by walking faster too. The victim can hear his footsteps now, and she breaks into a run. There's a real sense of danger because she's hampered by high heels. See if you can build it up and take it through to its climax.'

Theresa asked, 'How long has it to be?'

'Exactly sixty seconds. No more and no less.'

'Why?'

'Because that's how film music is organised. It has to fit into an exact time frame, and I'm going to play you an example of that.' He switched on the tape player, and they listened with total concentration to the final part of the pursuit. It was one of Frank Morrison's library scores, not written for a particular film, but it served Gavin's purpose.

After twenty minutes, he sent them on their way and welcomed the next group, which consisted of one female and.... His spirits ebbed. He knew the feeling of reward and success couldn't last for ever. One of the male students was Kevin McNamara.

Gavin ran through the introduction again, cautiously relieved that he was allowed to speak uninterrupted, until he was about to play the recording, and that was Kevin's cue to interrupt.

'Who wrote this music, and who did he write it for?'

'It's by Frank Morrison and it's a library score, which means that, on payment of a fee, anyone can use it.'

'So, how much did you have to pay for it?'

'I forget. It was quite a long time ago.' He thought that might be the end of it, but Kevin had other ideas.

'If you got it for teaching, why did you have to pay for it?'

'That's how the system works, Kevin. If you want something, you go to a shop and buy it.'

'You never give me a proper answer.'

'It may seem so, Kevin.' Twenty minutes was a very short space of time, and he had to get on with the tutorial. 'If you want to discuss the provision of educational resources,' he said, 'go and talk to Mr Best about it. He'd love to see you, and he's an expert on procurement and funding.'

'Right, I will.' Kevin opened the door to leave.

'Oh, Kevin?'

'What?'

'Try to keep it factual.'

The departing student slammed the door behind him, and one of the group said, 'Well done, Gavin.' The other agreed with him.

At lunchtime, Gavin walked the short distance to Robshaw's Tea Room, telling himself that if he ate a fairly hearty lunch, he had no need to cook when he returned to his flat at night. He ordered baked beans and sausages on toast with a poached egg on top. His meal arrived promptly, and he was enjoying it, when a voice asked, 'Are you feeding the creative force that lies within?'

He looked up and saw Leah. 'Hello,' he said, 'I'm giving myself a treat after a successful morning.'

'Do you mind if I join you?'

'Please do.' He noticed that she was no longer using a walking stick. 'Well done,' he said. 'No stick.'

She nodded. 'I can drive again. I'll save a fortune now I don't have to use taxis.'

The waitress came to the table. Leah said, 'A tuna salad and coffee, please.'

'You're making me feel guilty.'

'Good. You're like my dad,' she observed. 'He eats like a horse and shows nothing for it. It's the rest of us who have to be careful what we eat.'

'At the risk of sounding conventional,' he said, 'do you come here often?'

'Not really, and I'd no idea you'd be here, although I'm glad you are, because I've been wanting a word with you ever since the showdown at the Luvvie Corral.'

'Be my guest.'

'It's just that you said something about not wanting to offend anyone in that room.'

'As a rule, I try not to.'

'Okay, but what did you mean?'

'Just that.'

She sighed impatiently. 'You were talking about... sexual preferences, and you didn't want to offend anyone.' She began counting unnecessarily on her fingers. 'Vincent is straight, okay?'

'Yes.'

'Neil is too, so who were you afraid of offending?'

He closed his eyes in embarrassment. 'Not to put too fine a point on it,' he said, 'you.'

Disbelief made her shake her head. 'You think I'm a lesbian?'

A woman at the next table overheard her and turned away, embarrassed.

'I'm sorry, Leah. That was the impression I was given.'

The waitress arrived with her tuna salad, so they waited until she'd gone.

'Look,' he said, 'I really am sorry if I've got hold of the wrong end of the stick.' It was one of those moments when he wanted to become invisible.

'Whatever gave you that...? Just a minute. You said it was the impression you were given. Was it something Neil told you?'

'Yes.'

'That explains it.'

'Did he make the same mistake?'

'Not really.'

'I was obviously wrong. I can only apologise.'

'There's no need.'

'I should have realised. You're far too good-looking to be, you know, one of them.'

Her eyes grew wide with feigned shock. 'Gavin, how can you say that, with the Sex Discrimination Bill going through the House of Lords as we speak?' Smiling again, she shook her head and said, 'Look, when I came to the college, Neil tried it on with me and I let him know there was nothing doing. Now, as he's a legend in his own bedtime, it naturally follows that any woman who doesn't fancy him has to be either frigid or a lesbian. He placed me in the second category.'

He pushed his empty plate away and said, 'I still feel awful that I said what I did.'

'You were reacting to what you'd been told, and you wanted to avoid giving offence. That's all.' She laughed. 'It's quite funny, really.'

'I'm glad you think so.' It was a relief and quite unexpected. 'I must say,' he said, 'I still don't understand how Neil can expect to appeal to women, behaving as he does.'

'He doesn't behave like that when he's with women. He goes into a different act then. Basically, I don't think anyone knows what he's really like.'

'Clare told me he's okay when he stops posing.'

Leah smiled. 'Clare would find something good to say about

Jack the Ripper. With the possible exception of my mum, she's the sweetest-natured person I know.'

'Let's forget about Neil, then.'

'Let's,' she agreed.

'Can we meet soon? I have a number to show you, and it cries out for a dance routine. It's called "The Torture Chamber Charleston". At least, I hope it's a Charleston, but I'm sure you'll correct me if I'm wrong.'

'You'd have to change the title.'

'That's all right. "One-Step" or "Two-Step" would scan just as well.'

The idea seemed to appeal to her. 'I've got a ballet class at three o'clock, but I'm free until then.'

'The number is sung by King Philip the Second of Spain, and it's his last fling before being banished to the Underworld as an unrepentant sinner.' After a short introduction, he went into the chorus, which was unmistakably a Charleston.

'I like it,' said Leah when he'd finished. 'I can do plenty with that. Have you got the lyrics?'

'Here they are.' Gavin took a single sheet of paper from the top of the piano.

'Thanks.' She took it and read:

Torturing is quite the 'thing',
It's oh so trendy, yes, it's madly 'in',
And the branding irons have a fascinating ring,
When you're doin' the Torture Chamber Charleston.

Verse: Oh, I like to see a British tar tied neatly to the rack,
There's never been a better way to welcome Jolly Jack,
But the singular attraction that all the others lack,
Is the rhythm of the Torture Chamber Charleston!

Torturing etc

Verse: I like the iron maiden, with its positive embrace,
And I revel in the hopeless look upon the victim's face,
But the one pursuit that beats them all for beauty, poise and grace,
Is the rhythm of the Torture Chamber Charleston!

Torturing etc

Verse: I like the chains and manacles that hold the pris'ner still,
And I like the busy thumbscrews that bend him to my will,
But my favourite attraction and the greatest-ever thrill,
Is the rhythm of the Torture Chamber Charleston!

Torturing etc.
24 bars instrumental.

Verse: I hate the English sea-dogs, who the seven seas would take,
Such as Frobisher and Raleigh, and Effingham and Drake,
But my one remaining pleasure left bobbing in their wake,
Is the rhythm of the Torture Chamber Charleston!

Torturing etc.

'Twenty-four bars' instrumental,' she commented. 'That could be quite a spectacle. I think you've got something here, Gavin.'

'Thanks. We'll have to speak to Neil about it, but I wonder about dressing the victims in black body stockings and masks painted to look like skeletons.'

'Yes, skeletons dancing the Charleston. I like it.'

'Let's hope Neil will.'

'He should. It's outrageous enough to appeal to him.'

'Gavin, you ruined my morning.' Jonathan looked as if he might burst into tears. 'You sent a student to me....'

'Comrade Kevin, yes.'

'I couldn't get rid of him. He was in this office for at least an hour.'

'I hope you answered all his questions, Jonathan. He's quite insistent about that.'

Jonathan gave an impression of a safety valve about to blow. 'What is he doing here?'

'He wants to take a teaching diploma on the guitar so that he can pass on his musical skills to the downtrodden masses, presumably free of charge and without reference to composers with bourgeois connections.' He added for good measure, 'Especially those who used table napkins.'

Jonathan wasn't listening, locked as he was in his woeful experience. 'He described the organ as a propaganda weapon used by the Church in its despicable work of anaesthetising the downtrodden masses against their suffering, instead of joining the struggle against the capitalist oppressors.'

'I can see how that would offend you, Jonathan.' An attack on the Christian Church was one thing, but harsh words about the hallowed instrument amounted to sacrilege of the most heinous kind.

'Why did you send him to me, Gavin.' Jonathan's tone was reminiscent of Julius Caesar's anguished utterance, *Et tu, Brute?*

'I wanted to teach the rest of the class, but Kevin seems to find the concept irrelevant.' Out of interest, he asked, 'Did he accuse you of not listening to him?'

'Yes,' exploded Jonathan, 'about forty bloody times!'

'I thought he might.'

Jonathan made a visible attempt to relax. After a short while, he said, 'Gavin, we're short of students who are ready to give lunch-hour recitals, so I'm asking staff to help out. Will you do one?'

'Piano or clarinet?'

'I don't care.'

'I wouldn't normally do it. I'd far rather the students did them, but as there's no one available, and because you've had such an awful time, Jonathan, I'll put a programme together. How long is a lunch-hour recital?'

'Forty-five minutes. Thank you, Gavin.'

'You're welcome, Jonathan. Have a pleasant evening.'

As he left the office, Gavin thought he heard a sob. He smiled to himself and began to think about his next music number.

8

Faced with a class of eager students, Leah could only count herself fortunate.

'Now, *pliés*. Into second position. And one, and two, and three, and four, and five, and six, and seven... the third time, reverse the arm. Good.'

At the conclusion of the *barre* exercises, she walked over to one of the students and asked, 'What's your name?'

'Valerie Short, Miss Hinchcliffe.'

'Call me Leah. Now, Valerie, don't rotate your legs to that extent. You're not Mary Poppins.' She motioned the class not to laugh.

'No.'

'You're nervous, aren't you?'

The girl nodded.

'And you're trying too hard. I can understand that. Bring your legs back a touch. That's right.' Standing back, she addressed the whole class. 'It took a careless driver to end my dance career,' she told them. 'I could do nothing about it, but you can all lessen the risk of injury to yourselves by sticking to the rules and by treating your bodies with respect.' She gave the unfortunate Valerie a quick smile of encouragement, and was about to proceed with the class, when another student asked, 'When are the auditions for the show going to be held, Leah?'

'Not for some time, I'm afraid. We were short of a composer and lyricist until this term. Gavin's working as quickly as he can, but we have to be realistic.'

'What kind of music is it going to be?' The question came from a short, dark-haired girl, whose performance at the *barre* had been very promising.

'It's going to be a mixture of styles, apparently. As a matter of fact, I heard one of them, a Charleston, the other day.' The students looked at her with new interest.

The dark-haired girl asked, 'Will the auditions be open to anybody?'

'Absolutely everyone,' she confirmed. 'What's your name?'

'Christine Patchett.'

'Will you audition, Christine?'

'Yes.'

'Good. It's going to be an exciting show.' Gavin's early efforts had convinced her of that.

⌐∾⌐

Gavin was struggling. He had to write a song for Queen Elizabeth the First, who was bemoaning the fact that she'd been the Virgin Queen for far too long, and was now craving long-term male company. It was a difficult subject for a song, especially as, eager though she was, the celebrated queen would doubtless have in mind a special kind of man, a powerful man, a skilful and accomplished man; in fact, a super man.... That gave him an idea for a first line:

I'd like a superhero, flying in the face of fear,
Oh....

He needed something to do with zooming down to earth.

Oh, wouldn't such a man be heaven-sent?

Like her choice of man, it would do for the time being. He imagined that Good Queen Bess might become rather bored with Superman in his off-duty hours.

'I'd like a bold Sir Knight, slaying dragons left and right,
Superman is sometimes just Clark Kent.

Gavin was warming to the fickle queen, but what kind of man could depose the knight? He thought for a while, and wrote:

I'd like a Dalai Lama better than a knight in armour,
Never growing old in Shangri-La.

He looked at his ideas so far, and decided that, with short instrumental interludes, they were quite promising. He thought again, and wrote:

I'd like a circus clown, with laughing eyes and painted frown,
Laughs in Shangri-La are few and far.

It was time to be even sillier.

I'd like a movie star, better than a clown by far,
We could live the dream in Hollywood.

And then, disillusionment would return.

The men I'd like are oh, so many. Though movie stars are two a
penny,
Still I face eternal spinsterhood.

It had to end with just a hint of optimism.

Until now, there's no suggestion anyone will pop the question,
Hoping for the answer I've rehearsed.
So I'll keep my options open, stick around and go on hopin',
And I'll take the man that asks me first.

Satisfied for the time being with his progress, he put his work in his briefcase. He had a History of Music session with the External Diploma class in ten minutes.

On his way to his teaching room, he met Robert Cunningham, tutor for the new Foundation Course.

'Hello, Lowe,' he said. 'Has Jonathan asked you about a lunch-hour yet?' He seemed to be looking elsewhere.

'Yes, he has.'

'What are you going to play?'

'I don't know. I haven't decided yet whether to do it on the clarinet or the piano.'

Cunningham gave him a strange, darting look before averting his gaze once more. 'Should you choose to do it on the piano,' he said, 'can you avoid Schumann's *Davidsbündlertänze*? That's what I'm playing.'

'I'll regard it as your exclusive domain.'

'Thank you.'

'It's no sacrifice.' He was actually quite fond of the Schumann, but he wouldn't have chosen it for a recital. He continued to Room 6 in time to greet his class.

'Good morning,' he said. 'Because we're looking at sonata form in Analysis, I'm going to begin with some of the composers of the early Classical period, when the form first appeared.

'Haydn's life spanned the Classical period. He was born in seventeen-thirty-two and he died in eighteen-oh-nine. As well as becoming known, as you're probably aware, as the Father of the Symphony, he is remembered for his work in various other forms. In those days, of course, musicians worked under the patronage of either the aristocracy or the Church, and Haydn, being no exception, spent most of his career working for Prince Esterhàzy and his family. He put his originality of style down to his enclosed existence, insulated as he was from external....' He realised that Kevin was about to speak. 'Yes, Kevin? I hope it's about Haydn.'

'Are you saying it was a good thing for composers to work for the aristocracy?'

Several members of the class groaned, but Gavin replied to the question. 'If you were listening, you would have heard me say that Haydn gave his enclosed existence as the reason for his originality. It was a simple statement of fact.'

'No, you're saying it was a good thing.'

'Kevin, go and talk to Mr Best about patronage. He's an expert on it.' Jonathan was probably the most patronising bugger Gavin knew, so it seemed roughly appropriate.

'I'm going to complain about you.'

'You do surprise me, Kevin.'

A student voice said, 'Get lost, Kevin.'

Another, the girl who had complimented Gavin earlier on his patience, said, 'Yes, bugger off, Kevin, and then we can all get a share of Gavin's time.' The others joined in the chorus.

Kevin left the room, slamming the door and causing the room to shake.

'This is as good a time as any,' said Gavin, 'to listen to Haydn's *"Farewell" Symphony*. We'll continue with his life after we've heard it.'

Two days later, Leah arrived at the Recital Hall for Robert Cunningham's lunch-time recital, during which he was to play the cycle of miniatures that Schumann had dubbed 'The Dance of David's Followers.' The programme notes told her that the title was an allusion to the biblical David's fight against the Philistines. It seemed that Schumann saw himself leading a similar assault on the philistines of the 19th century, and Leah applauded his motive, although she would reserve judgement of his music until she'd heard it.

She found Gavin seated near the back, and joined him.

'Hello, Gavin.'

'Leah, how nice to see you. Do you come to these things regularly?'

'Only if they appeal.' She would have said more, but Jonathan Best had arrived, and he seemed to require Gavin's attention. He was looking more relaxed than usual. He acknowledged Leah briefly before addressing Gavin.

'Ah, Gavin,' he said, 'this is the first time I've seen you since you sent Kevin McNamara to me.'

'Yes, he was absent today.'

Jonathan smiled. 'As he will be every day from now until the end of time. He was most abusive, you know.'

'Kevin? No, really?'

'Yes, and I lost my temper. I shouted at him.'

'We're all human, Jonathan. Don't let it weigh too heavily on your conscience.'

Almost gleefully, Jonathan said, 'He's gone. He decided to apply elsewhere.'

'And he and I were just getting to know each other.' Gavin couldn't resist asking, 'Did he discuss the morality of noble patronage with you, Jonathan? That was the purpose of his visit.'

'No, he didn't. Anyway, I must leave you.' Jonathan continued to the end of the row, where he joined one of his organist colleagues.

Gavin turned to Leah and said, 'I suppose Jonathan could best be described as suavely ill-mannered.'

'I can see you're getting to know him. What's Robert Cunningham like?'

'I've never heard him play. He's a bit weird, actually. He avoids eye contact during conversation, which is disconcerting, and he addresses me as "Lowe". I suppose it's difficult for him to feel at ease with human beings and other alien species. Anyway, we shall see what he's like as a pianist.'

A few minutes later, Robert Cunningham swept in and took an exaggerated bow before taking his seat at the piano.

Thereafter, both Gavin and Leah averted their gaze, because the spectacle was too grotesque for them to witness. Cunningham's playing was quite good. The problem was the facial contortions and exaggerated arm movements that accompanied it, presenting a hideous distraction from Schumann's music.

When it was over, Gavin took Leah outside.

'I couldn't believe it,' he said. 'Every note was a new sensation. It was truly emetic.'

Leah was laughing. 'It's the first time I've seen dance incorporated into piano-playing,' she said. 'He could teach my students something about *ports de bras*.'

'Come again?'

' "Carriage of the arms",' she translated.

'Anyway, that's made my decision for me,' he said.

'Are you going in for ballet as well?'

'No, I'm going to do my lunch-hour on the piano. I have to show the students that it's possible to play and sit still at the same time without resorting to co-ordination therapy.'

'I'll look forward to that. When is it?'

'In two weeks' time.' Remembering something else, he said, 'I've written another number for the show.'

'Oh, Gavin,' she said, putting her hand on his arm, 'your output would pose a threat to Ernie Wise. What's the number?'

'It's for the scene where Good Queen Bess decides that virginity is overrated, and she's trying to decide what kind of man she wants.'

'It doesn't sound like something that calls out for a dance sequence, but I'd like to hear it, anyway. What's the next one going to be?'

'A set piece with dancing and vocal chorus. It's the scene in Cleopatra's bathroom.'

'I remember now.' She raised an eyebrow to say, 'Are we allowed to do that?'

'It'll be very correct,' he assured her.

'What kind of dance do you envisage?'

'Tap.' Resisting the urge to make the bathroom connection, he asked, 'Did you ever see the harem scene in *Roman Scandals*?'

'Eddie Cantor and "Keep Young and Beautiful"? Is that the kind of thing you have in mind?' Her enthusiasm was growing already.

'Yes, but it's more along the lines of, Keep Clean and You're in with a Chance, although not in those exact words. Incidentally, on the subject of tap. How's your knee, now you've jettisoned the walking stick?'

'Slow progress, but thanks for asking. I shan't be teaching tap, by the way. There's a part-time lecturer who comes in to do that.'

'Good, but it is improving?'

'Slowly, as I said. I'm doing *pliés* to strengthen the joint, but I had to stop after twenty this morning.'

'Forgive my ignorance, but—'

'What is a *plié*? It's a *barre* exercise. Keeping your back straight, you dip down, flexing your knees outward. I'd show you, but it might create a spectacle here.

'It sounds like the policeman's stretch.'

'You know,' she said, 'it could easily have been called *l'étirement du gendarme*, but I think I prefer *plié*. Anyway, I'm looking forward to your bathroom scene.'

9

Now fit to drive again, Leah headed home for the weekend. It had been a relatively quiet journey, and now she turned into Easingthorpe, where her parents lived, and drove along the main street, past the marketplace and the Shearer's Arms. She saw Wendy Albright leaving the supermarket where she worked, and pulled into the kerbside to offer her a lift.

'Thanks, Leah.' Wendy put her bag of shopping between her feet and closed the door. 'How's your knee?'

'It's getting there, thanks, Wendy. How's the pantomime coming along?' Wendy's famous assets were currently concealed by flared trousers and a maxi coat.

'It's not bad, but we need to find another Tom. She's broken her leg, and it's going to be in plaster for at least two months. My cousin had hers in plaster for thirteen weeks. I couldn't cope with that. Could you?'

'I did, when I was sixteen, but never mind.' Leah was about to ask a silly question, but remembered in time that Tom was Dick Whittington's cat. She said, 'It shouldn't be too difficult, finding one. There must be lots of kids who are keen to audition.'

'Yes, about thirty of 'em. Your mum's holding the auditions tomorrow morning. Just think of it, all those pushy mothers. I couldn't do it, myself. I'd go bananas in no time. The kids are bad enough, but their mothers are worse.'

'Poor Mum.' She had to say something, or Wendy was likely to go on indefinitely.

'Like I say, it's really good of your mum and dad to do this. They must be busy enough with everything else.'

'Oh, they thrive on it, Wendy.' Leah turned into Yoredale Close and parked the Mini outside number 4.

Wendy picked up her shopping. 'Thanks for the lift, Leah.'

'You're welcome.'

'Is Martin still at home?' It was more than a casual question.

'I doubt it. You know he has a flat in Leeds, don't you?'

'Yes, I'd seen him around. I just wondered. "Bye.' She got out and closed the door, leaving Leah to wonder if Martin would ever muster the nerve to ask Wendy out. She locked her car and let herself into the house.

Seeing no sign of her mum, Leah imagined she must have taken Rhea for a walk or maybe gone shopping. Presently, however, she heard footsteps on the stairs, and her mum came down. With a broad smile, she held out her arms to hug her daughter.

'How's the knee?'

'Much better, thanks. Look, no stick.'

'Lovely. Sit down and I'll make some tea.'

'I'll make it, Mum.'

'No. Sit down.'

Leah sat down obediently while her mum went into the kitchen. She called out, 'Where's Rhea?'

'At the studio with your dad. She potters around quite happily while he's working. He talks to her all the time, you know, not that she understands a word he says, but it's all attention.'

Presently, her mum brought in the tea things, putting the tray down on the coffee table. She asked, 'Do you remember Derek and Joan Cresswell? Joan helped your dad get established with the equestrian population when we came to Easingthorpe.'

'Yes, I remember them. What have they been up to?'

'It's their ruby wedding on the eighth of November, and they're having a big celebration at Nidderdale Cricket Club. They've hired the "Dalesmen", and the rest of us are invited.'

'How many years is a ruby wedding, Mum?'

'Forty.' She took a card, presumably the invitation, from its envelope to show her.

'Forty years,' said Leah, 'almost as long as Rudolf Hess served.'

'Don't be awful, Leah.'

Leah read the invitation. 'It says I can bring someone,' she said.

'Have you got someone to bring?' Her mum's eyes were suddenly full of interest. She was an inveterate matchmaker, always ready to make plans for her daughter. The war had delayed her marriage until she was twenty-three, but she maintained that, at twenty-four, Leah had no excuse for being single.

'I told a new colleague I'd bring him to the next gig,' she said, taking the cup of tea her mother offered. 'His clarinet teacher at school played with some of the West End dance bands before the war, and that kind of thing is infectious, as you know.'

'Your dad will enjoy meeting him, then.'

'And so will you, but just forget about wedding bells, Mum. They're not on the agenda.' Before her mother could protest, she said, 'I'll tell you what is, though. I gave Wendy Albright a lift home from the supermarket, and she was keen to know if Martin was still at home.'

'Don't you go teasing Martin, Leah.'

'I wouldn't dream of it, although I can't help thinking that the pantomime could turn out to be a trifle embarrassing for both of them.'

Her mum gave her a stern look and said, 'It will if you have anything to do with it.'

'Not me,' said Leah innocently, 'but you know how Dick Whittington usually loses his cat and has to go searching for him?'

'Yes.' It was a guarded response.

'Well, when Wendy comes down from the stage, into the audience, and asks if anyone has seen her pussy, Martin will be able to say, "No, but I've seen everything else." '

'Leah, behave yourself.' Her mum was nevertheless trying to stifle her amusement.

'How is Martin now?' Her concern was real as well as timely.

'He's a lot better. Your dad went with him to the inquest. It wasn't too awful, and the family of the boy who was killed were sympathetic towards Martin because of what he'd experienced.'

'Hey, that was noble of them.'

'It was. Maybe Martin can settle down now.'

'I hope so.'

The sound of an engine caused Leah to look out of the window. 'Oh,' she said, 'it's Dad and Rhea.' The Avenger estate car drew to a halt outside, and Leah's father got out, followed by Rhea close at his heels. A moment later, they were in the house, with Rhea welcoming everyone as old friends and prolonging the occasion as best she could.

'How's my lovely daughter?'

Leah stood up to receive a hug. 'All the better for being here, Dad.'

'How about you, SP? Good day?'

'Very useful, Freddy.' She accepted a kiss before telling him, 'Leah's met a young man who's keen on dance music. She's going to bring him to the Cresswells' ruby wedding.' She handed her husband a cup of tea.

'I've told you, Mum. Put your wedding hat back in its box. There's nothing to it.'

'I'll buy a new hat for your wedding, Leah; in fact, a whole, new outfit.'

'And I'll be expected to pay for it,' said her dad, 'so take your time, daughter mine. We're not hurrying you into anything.' The humour in his eyes said everything.

'I'm holding auditions tomorrow morning, Leah,' said her mother, conveniently changing the subject. 'We need a new Tom for the pantomime.'

'I know. Wendy told me about it.'

'And I'm working,' said her father.

'That's all right. I'll go and see Elaine and Janice. I imagine Bailey will be working too. He usually is.'

'That'll be nice, Leah. Janice asks about you all the time.'

Suddenly, and for no obvious reason, Leah had a brainwave. 'Mum,' she asked, 'can Wendy Albright dance?'

'Do you mean on stage?'

'No, I'm talking about ballroom dancing.'

'She danced with your dad at the last Yoredale Players' party.'

Leah's father feigned a look of guilt. 'You weren't meant to see that, SP. I thought Wendy and I had covered our tracks with that episode.'

'Don't be silly, Freddy. She can dance, can't she?'

'Yes, she's quite good.'

'Why do you ask, Leah?'

She gave her mum a sideways look and said, 'I'm wondering – and don't go off half-cocked. Please hear me out – I'm wondering if Martin would like to take her to the ruby wedding party.'

'Leah, how many times must I tell you? You mustn't tease him.'

'I'm not going to tease him, Mum. I'll be gentle and I'll put it to him as a sister should. I think it would do him a power of good, and Wendy's keen, as you know.'

'I think it might be good for him,' agreed her father, 'but you'll have to be very careful how you put it to him.'

Leah knew that well enough, but she made no comment. Instead, changed the subject by asking, 'Where's Rhea?'

'She's playing in the garden,' said her father. 'When she's not listening appreciatively to my efforts on the piano, which she often does, she potters in the garden.'

'Of course.' Now she thought about it, the other Scotties had always been happy to amuse themselves.

'She plays with her plant pots,' he explained. 'It's a kind of pottering.'

'She doesn't chew them, does she?' They weren't the cleanest objects a dog could find.

'She wouldn't dream of it,' said her mother. 'She arranges them in rows and then rearranges them until she's satisfied. It can take quite a long time.'

Leah shook her head in disbelief. 'I learn something new every time I come home,' she said.

───※───

Leah found her godmother and Janice at home, as she'd expected. Janice was the first to welcome her, hugging and kissing her as if they'd not seen each other for a very long time. Like many people with Down's syndrome, Janice was very affectionate. She was also very fond of Leah, whom she called her 'cousin'.

'Janice was wondering if you'd come, Leah,' said Elaine, greeting her with a kiss, 'and I'm glad you did.'

'Is Bailey at work?'

'Yes. I'll make coffee, shall I?'

'That's a good idea.' Leah returned her attention to Janice. 'And what have you been up to, Janice?' The question was unnecessary; she could see Janice's transistor radio with its back off and battery hanging from the lead that connected it to whatever mystery existed inside.

'It's broke.'

'Broken, is it? It's a shame Martin isn't here. I bet he could mend it.'

Janice's eyes opened wide. 'Is he coming?'

'No, he's in Leeds.'

'Are you going to tell him to come?'

'No, Janice, I don't tell him to do things. He has to please himself.'

'Well, who's going to mend this, then?' The question came with a note of asperity that was usually a warning sign.

'I don't know, but if you're very good, I might be able to do something with it.' Leah picked up the radio to examine it. The case was cracked, possibly because of ill-treatment at some stage when Janice's patience had snapped, but that wasn't bound to be the cause of the malfunction.

'I tried to mend it,' said Janice.

'Yes, I can see that.' She could also see that one of the battery's terminals was disconnected. It was a PP3, one of those small, rectangular batteries that needed a special connector. Twisting the battery, she lined up the disconnected terminal with its plug and squeezed them together. Immediately, the radio hissed and crackled.

'It's working again,' said Janice, making grab for it just as her mother came into the room with the coffee.

'You need to tune it,' Leah told her.

'I know.' Janice seized the tuning knob.

'You'll have to be gentle or it might break again.' Leah replaced the cover on the battery compartment and turned the knob slowly until the condenser picked up a station. She had no idea which, but that didn't seem to matter to Janice. The main thing was that it was working again.

'It's working,' she told her mother.

'Did Leah mend it for you?'

'Yes.'

'What are you going to say to Leah?'

'I don't know.' She was fiddling with the tuning knob again.

'Leah just did something for you. What should you say?'

Janice concentrated, and then, as realisation dawned, threw her arms round Leah's neck and said, 'I love you, Leah.'

'That's nice, but there's something else you should say. First, you say, "Please", and then...'

'Thank you.'

'Good girl.'

Janice proceeded to monopolise Leah for the rest of the morning, but it was only to be expected, and it was no trouble.

Leah arrived home keen to hear about the result of her mother's efforts.

'I've cast Tom,' she said. 'She's a nice girl from the junior school. I don't think we'll have any problems with her.'

'The previous Tom created a lot of problems,' said her dad. 'For a ten-year-old, she'd have put any diva to shame.'

'I don't stand for any of that,' said Leah. 'If they want to be temperamental, I ask them who they're trying to impress, because they certainly don't impress me. They sometimes sulk for a while, but it usually does the trick.'

Her mum's thoughts seemed to be elsewhere, because she asked, 'When are you going to speak to Martin, Leah?'

'I'll write to him. It's the best way.'

'Are you sure?' Her mum sounded doubtful.

'I'm convinced of it. When he was at the polytechnic, he always had more to say in his letters than he ever did on the phone or face to face.'

'Don't press him, Leah. You know what he's like.'

'I shan't, Mum. He'll most likely tell me to mind my own business, in which case I shall, but it's worth a try.' She was hoping that might allay her mum's fears, but she was wrong.

'The main thing is you mustn't tease him. I mean all that stuff about Wendy not drawing her curtains. It's unkind.'

'I mentioned it to him once, Mum, that's all. I was only having a bit of fun with you, and I'm sorry if I worried you. You have to remember, though, he's my brother, and I love him just as much as you do. That's why I'm trying to help him.'

Her dad, who had been quiet throughout the conversation, said, 'You know, we have to stop talking about Martin as if there's something wrong with him. He's shy, that's all.'

'That's all,' agreed Leah. It was easier to agree, because she really didn't know the answer.

10

Gavin held the door to admit a stocky man with shoulder-length, dark hair and a droopy moustache. He wore jeans and a denim jacket.

'Good morning, everyone,' said Gavin. 'Before I introduce our visitor, let me ask you how many of you saw the TV series *Do Buck Up?*' It was a safe question, as the school-based comedy series had been highly popular with young viewers.

A general look of puzzlement gave way to a number of hands raised cautiously at first, and then others joined them with increasing confidence.

'Good, because this is Frank Morrison, the composer who wrote the theme music for it. He also wrote the library score that I played for you as an example. He's been looking at your work, and he's very kindly agreed to come and talk to you about it.' They didn't need to know about the visiting lecturer's fee of £20 that Gavin had managed, with some difficulty, to wring out of Jonathan Best. With a gesture of invitation to Frank, he stepped back.

'Good morning,' said Frank. 'This takes me back to when I was a music student.' He gave them a look of mock reproach and added, 'It wasn't as long ago as you're thinking. Gavin will tell you that, because we were students at the same time, and that's why I was so pleased when he asked me to look at your work.' He opened his briefcase and took out their manuscripts, which he placed on one of the desks on the front row.

'I'm not going to talk about them individually, because I've attached my comments to each manuscript, and you can read them in due course. In the meantime, though, I'm going to make some general observations.' He took out some notes he'd made, and began.

'Generally speaking, I'm impressed with what I've seen. You've gone about this task enthusiastically and taken a lot of care over it. Some of you have even annotated your manuscript, showing what happens and when.' Almost apologetically, he explained, 'It doesn't actually work like that in practice. The composer is given a timing sheet that lists all those things and says where the music has to go – I'll leave an example of one with Gavin for you to look at – but you weren't expected to know about timing sheets, so it shows clear and imaginative thinking on your part.' He consulted his notes again.

'Something to bear in mind is that you're not creating a self-contained miniature, so there's no need to write an introduction and then sign off like Beethoven, with a series of repeated chords, unless, of course, those chords accompany something, like a significant and repeated action.' He illustrated his point by pretending to hit something or someone with a series of heavy blows. 'More often than not, though, think of the music rather as a fragment torn from a longer score, and remember that the most important thing is that the music supplements what is happening on the screen.' He took the top two manuscripts and separated them so that he could read the students' names.

'Are Linda Bower and David Turner here?'

Two hands went up.

'I know I said I wasn't going to talk about manuscripts individually, but there are two that deserve special mention. Linda and David, I was very impressed with yours. You both went about this task in a professional way. You even attached a programme, rather like a timing sheet; in fact, Linda, you listed your exact timings. David, you stipulated a metronome mark, which was also helpful. Well done, everyone, but particularly David and Linda.'

'Thank you, Frank,' said Gavin. 'We're grateful for your advice and encouragement.' He put his hands together as a hint to the students, and they responded with a round of applause.

'Thank you,' said Frank. 'Now, if you have any questions, I'll do my best to answer them.'

One hand went aloft immediately. It belonged to David Turner.

'Frank, when they record your scores, do you conduct them yourself?'

'That's a good question. Yes, most composers do nowadays. At one time, you see, the film studios used established and celebrated composers, such as Sir William Walton, Sir Arthur Bliss or Ralph Vaughan-Williams, who'd received most, if not all, of their musical education at Oxford or Cambridge Universities, so they were un-tutored in the artisan practice of conducting in a recording studio. That's why, if you watch a film of a certain vintage, after the com-poser's credit, you'll see "Conducted by Muir Matheson" or another of the in-house musical directors. More recently, however, they've taken to using people like me, who've studied at one of the colleges or academies and been taught about conducting in the real world. Does that answer your question, David?'

'Yes, thanks, Frank.'

He answered two more questions, and then it was time to break for lunch. Gavin saw the students out and said to Frank, 'We could have lunch at the pub, or one of superior quality at the café.'

'I have to work this afternoon,' said Frank, 'so I don't want to fall asleep. Can we make it the café?'

'By all means. One of their celebrated dishes is pork sausages and beans on toast with a poached egg on top.'

Frank groaned. 'You were talking dirty with the sausages and beans,' he said, 'but the poached egg is just shameless seduction.' Possibly as a distraction from the tantalising prospect, he looked around him and said, 'It's a great setting for a music school.'

'Very nice,' agreed Gavin, 'but its future is threatened.'

'Oh, no. It seems to follow you round.'

'It does,' he agreed. 'Meanwhile, I'm co-operating with the Drama and Dance School to produce a musical that they can stage for one night at one of the London theatres. They're hop-ing that with a right publicity it'll encourage more students to come here.'

Frank considered that for a moment, and asked, 'How does that work, I mean with the theatre?'

'Most of them have one night, usually Sunday or Monday, when nothing's happening, and that's when students, stage schools and so, on can use them.'

'Well, I never knew that.'

Gavin pointed to the next building and said, 'This is it. Robshaw's Café.'

'Hooray. Lead me to the sausages, beans and poached egg.'

'They do other things as well.'

'How dare they?'

They found a table and pretended, for appearances' sake, to read the menu. When the waitress came, Gavin ordered for them both.

'You went down well this morning, Frank,' he said. 'I'm grateful.'

'Think nothing of it. In any case, the fee is most welcome.'

'How are things going?'

Frank shrugged modestly. 'It's picking up. I can't turn my nose up at anything that comes along, but that's life. I even wrote some pop ballads recently. Cindy Freeman recorded them.'

'What are they called?'

'Go on, make me cringe. "Something Great is Happening" and "Stay With Me".'

'It's honest work, Frank. Do you use a pseudonym?'

'Of course I do. I don't want the whole world to know I'm desperate.' He leaned forward confidentially and said, 'I do it under the name William H Bonney.'

'Billy the Kid,' observed Gavin. 'Of course, your heart was always in the Wild West.'

'It still is, pardner.' Frank gave his lawman's moustache a tweak.

'Ah, here comes the grub.'

In a kind of daze, Frank watched the waitress put the food on the table.

She asked, 'Can I get you anything else?'

'No, thank you,' he murmured. 'Everything's perfect.'

'You know, Frank,' said Gavin, shaking him out of his trance, 'it doesn't feel like five years since we were at the College.'

'Maybe I notice the years more than you, Gavin. If you remember, my grand exit was in response to a pregnant girlfriend and irate future in-laws.'

'How is the family?'

'Helen's fine, and Katherine is four now. She'll start school next year.' With his former trance-like expression, he cut into a sausage. 'She wants to play every instrument in the orchestra. I'll leave it a year or two before I do anything about it.' He winced. 'Then I'll cop it from the in-laws. They already think I'm a bad influence on her.'

Gavin remembered the situation from earlier conversations. 'You know,' he said, 'with your in-law problem, you could do stand-up comedy.'

'Except it's no bloody joke. I'm not kidding, Gavin. Helen's mother has devoted so much of her life to disapproval, mainly with me in mind, that she has permanent, radiating lines on her upper lip, so that it looks like a cat's arse on a stormy night. And her father's as bad. He keeps asking me when I'm going to get a proper job.'

'They just don't understand, do they?' Gavin had just seen Leah at the entrance. He beckoned to her and said, 'Come and join us.'

'I don't want to intrude.'

'It's all right,' Gavin told her. 'We're not in love or anything like that.'

'No,' said Frank, pouting, 'we're just wanton, aren't we, Gav?'

'Leah, meet Frank Morrison, composer and browbeaten son-in-law. Frank, this is Leah Hinchcliffe, dance *suprema*.'

Frank stood up to shook hands with her.

'Frank came in today to talk to the students,' explained Gavin.

'And to do Gavin's marking for him,' added Frank. 'He's on his own tomorrow. I think he'll be all right.'

'Weren't you at college together?'

'And school,' said Gavin.

Leah recalled an earlier conversation. 'And you had a teacher who'd played with some of the West End bands before the war, right?'

'*Two* teachers,' said Frank. 'Mr Hutchins, known as "Hutch", taught Gavin, and Mr Barraclough, who allows me to call him "Norman" nowadays, taught me for a while until they got a specialist trumpet teacher. Norman played on a transatlantic liner at one time.'

'That must have been wonderful.'

'Leah's dad has a dance band, Frank.'

Frank waited while Leah gave her order to the waitress, and then asked, 'What kind of music does he play?'

'A little bit of forties and fifties, but mainly the music of the golden age.'

'Good for him. The best things have to be preserved.'

'I think he sees it as his mission when he's not photographing animals.'

Frank looked at his watch and said, 'I'll have to go, I'm afraid. I'll give you something for the bill, Gavin.'

'No, leave that to me.' Gavin stood up to shake his hand. 'Thanks for coming, Frank.'

'It was no trouble. Thanks for lunch. Keep in touch.' He shook hands again with Leah. 'Nice to meet you, Leah.'

'Me too, Frank.'

Leah watched him go. 'Nice chap,' she said.

'Yes, he can give the wrong impression with that floor-length hair and Wyatt Earp moustache. He's been like that since the sixties, but if you ask me, he only maintains the image to annoy his in-laws.'

'If he's as clever as you say, it doesn't matter what he looks like.'

Leah's prawn salad arrived. When the waitress was gone, she said, 'I have an invitation for you. My dad's band has a gig at Nidderdale Cricket Club on the eighth of next month. It's a ruby wedding celebration and my family are all invited. I can take someone, so how about it?'

'Thanks, Leah. I'd really like to hear the band. There's just one problem.'

'What's that?'

'I can't dance. I never learned how.'

'I'll give you a crash course. In the time we've got, I could teach you the waltz, the foxtrot and the quickstep, at least.'

Suddenly, he felt shy. 'I think you'll find I have two left feet.'

'Don't worry, Gavin. By the time I've finished with you, your feet will be so interchangeable they'll each have an identity crisis.'

'I believe you. When do we start? This afternoon?'

'I'm free after three.'

75

'Me too, and after that I'll nurse my bruises and make a start on Cleopatra's bathroom scene.'

A few days later, Leah received a reply from Martin, telling her to stop interfering. She wasn't surprised.

11

'What shall we do while we wait for Neil?' Leah stood with Gavin outside Neil's office.

'You could read this,' suggested Gavin, handing her two sheets of paper. 'It's hot off Clare's typewriter.'

'Oh, the bathroom scene. I've been looking forward to this.' Leah took the lyrics and read:

CLEOPATRA:

INTRO:There's a time when girls decline to be at home to callers,
Whether social, trade or special deals from CORGI gas installers.
Anyone who tries to phone will find his call rejected,
Bath-time is a sacred rite that has to be respected!

If you want to look the part,
This is where you have to start.
It's the place where health and beauty really begin.
Honey, clove and rose divine,
Cedarwood and sage combine,
In your bath to cleanse and purify your skin!

CHORUS OF SLAVE GIRLS:

In your bathtub you must go,
Pour the eucalyptus 'so',
It's the only way to be completely appealing.
Honeycomb and asses' milk,
Make your skin as smooth as silk.

It's the force that gives a girl that powerful feeling.

FIRST SLAVE GIRL [aside to audience]:

Cleopatra hankered after Mark Antonio,
Truth to tell, she loved the smell of his cologn-io.

SECOND SLAVE GIRL:

Aphrodite welcomed nightly gods with citrus scented,
No BO, because, you know, it hadn't been invented!

CHORUS OF SLAVE GIRLS:

Take the soap and water way,
Let your worries float away,
Make your bid to be the most sensational cutie!
Get yourself into the tub!
Give yourself an oatmeal scrub!
It's the only way to keep your natural beauty!

[CHANT, alla cheer leaders] Grab a sponge and take the plunge,
you know you really ought ta!
Turn the taps on, bathing caps on! Leap into the water!

DANCE ROUTINE 24 BARS

CLEOPATRA & SLAVE GIRLS:

Take the soap and water way,
Let your worries float away,
Make your bid to be the most sensational cutie!
Get yourself into the tub!
Give yourself an oatmeal scrub!
[CHANT] Time is precious, don't delay, get your clothes off right
away!
[BIG FINISH] It's the only way to keep your natural beauty!

'I like it, Gavin,' she said, handing it back. 'We can do a lot with that. I like the look of the music as well, although it stretches my modest ability on the piano.'

'I'll record it for you. All the dance numbers will have to be recorded, anyway.'

'True. If only we could record Neil and use that instead of the real thing,' she said, looking past Gavin.

Gavin turned and saw Neil approaching. 'If only,' he agreed.

'Good morning, dearies.' Neil caught a look from Gavin, and said, 'Butch company excepted, of course. Come into my parlour.' He unlocked the door and let them into his office, where, with rehearsed carelessness, he flicked the switch on the electric kettle and poured three measures of ground coffee into a cafetiere.

'Now,' he said, launching himself into his chair, 'how far on are we with the music, and can we start auditions yet?'

' "Cleopatra's Bathroom Scene", and, if Leah's in agreement, I'd say we can certainly make a start.' Gavin handed the lyrics to Neil, who read them, finally signalling his approval by smacking the paper with the back of his hand.

'Gavin lov... Gavin,' he said, 'this is just what's needed. Did any ideas about staging come to you while you were writing it?'

'There has to be a bath, or at least something that looks like one, and I see Cleopatra in a bathrobe. At some stage, she'll doff the robe and get into the bath. I imagine slaves could hold up two towels, one in front and one behind her while she does that, and then we'll need a bubble machine to cover her and disguise the fact that she's wearing a swimsuit or bikini.'

'Does she need to wear a swimsuit, I mean, if she's going to be covered in bubbles?'

Leah sighed. 'Neil, these are vulnerable young people. You can't ask a girl to appear naked in front of her fellow students.'

'I bet some of them would do it.'

'We're doing this for publicity,' she reminded him, 'but not the kind we'd get by exploiting young people.'

'All right, but why two towels? Wouldn't one be enough?'

'It's to shield her from the boxes and circles,' explained Gavin.

'Of course. Silly me. Right, auditions. Shall we compare diaries?'

He produced his with a grand gesture. Leah and Gavin opened theirs with a similar flourish.

'Oh, for goodness' sake,' protested Neil.

~⁂~

Leah and Gavin went to the café for lunch. Leah asked, 'Was it the Eddie Cantor number that made you score the bathroom scene as a Hollywood-type set piece?'

'Partly. It was on television recently. Did you see it?'

'Yes.'

'Frank and I were talking about it. It was his suggestion, actually.'

'Of course, you and he go back a long way, don't you?'

'We were at infant school together.'

She laughed. 'I can imagine you two as mixed infants.'

'Actually,' he explained, 'I'm a year older than Frank, so we didn't exactly play together in the sand pit, but we knew each other. He and his sister Penny used to come round to my house quite often. One thing we had in common was that we'd both lost our dads when we were little.'

'How awful.'

'I went out with Penny for a while. We were fifteen, I believe. It didn't happen when we were infants.'

Leah regarded him seriously. 'I'm glad you cleared that up, Gavin. What happened to make you go your separate ways?'

'She dropped me in favour of a lad called Tim Renshaw. They're married now. He was her dancing partner, so I suppose it made sense to them.'

'But not to you?' She ran her eye down the menu.

'No, I was distraught. I went home that day undecided whether to switch the telly on or phone the Samaritans. In the end, the telly won, because Blue Peter had a new cat, called Jason.'

'And so you bounced back.'

'I have to say, though, Penny's a great girl. They were on *Come Dancing*, you know.'

'Were they?'

'They were Northern Region Quickstep Champions.'

'They must have been pretty good.'

The waitress appeared at their table. Leah ordered a chicken salad and waited for Gavin to decide.

'Bangers and mash, please.' As the waitress left them, he explained, 'I eat a hearty lunch so that I don't have to cook for myself at night.'

'You eat heartily, all right,' she agreed, 'but not all that healthily.' She waved the subject aside, saying, 'That's your affair, though. It's not for me to criticise.'

'No, it's not, Leah. How dare you? Anyway, tell me about the pantomime your dad's producing.'

'It's Dick Whittington, as I told you, and there was a crisis last week. Dick's cat broke a leg, and my mum had to audition thirty kids for the part. I imagine most of the rats would rather be Tom.'

'No one wants to be cast as a baddy, Leah,' he said, adding, 'or an unhealthy eater, for that matter.' In a martyred tone, he said, 'It's wounding to be told a thing like that, but I'm a stoic. I can take it. Anyway, who's coming to the ruby wedding do?'

'My dad, obviously, my mum and possibly my brother Martin, but he's not bound to be there. He's painfully shy. I tried to fix him up with female company for the event, but he's not keen on the idea.'

'Can he dance?' Since his first tutorial with Leah, the subject had seldom been far from Gavin's thoughts.

'Yes, my mum taught him. The difficulty is in getting him to ask someone to dance with him.'

'Poor chap. Shyness is an awful thing. Believe it or not, Frank used to be shy until he learned to control it.' His thoughts moved on and he said, 'It's not as hard as I imagined. Dancing, I mean, but I can't get the hang of leading. I'm all right as long as I've got you to prompt me, but I'm not ready to take control.'

'Don't worry.' She smiled at his uncertainty. 'Stay in the after cockpit for now. If I'm not available, my mum will steer you round the floor.'

'What was that about a cockpit?'

'It's just something my dad says. He has lots of silly expressions.'

Gavin was looking thoughtful.

'A penny for them,' she suggested.

'I was thinking of your mum and dad. They sound like whole people.'

'What do you mean?'

'Just that some people need to be propped up occasionally, but your parents sound whole and self-reliant.'

'My dad says my mum lifted him and propped him up when he was going through a terrible time, after he lost his home and family during the war, and he only survived the Long March, as they call it, from the prison camp in Poland, because she'd given him a reason for surviving.'

'She sounds wonderful.'

'She's got a lot going for her,' agreed Leah. She smiled guiltily and said, 'She's so sweet and kind that I feel awful sometimes, when I've teased her. She doesn't deserve it.' She told him what she'd said to Martin about Wendy Albright, and how she'd carried on teasing her mother with it.

'You're right, Leah. It really was too bad of you.'

'I know, but I bet you wouldn't mind staying at my parents' house now, and sleeping in the front bedroom.'

'Of course I wouldn't, now you've whetted my appetite.' He considered the possibility and asked, 'Is she quite a big girl, this Wendy Albright?'

'She's tall and size twelve-ish. Her main attribute, and the one that got her the part of Dick Whittington, is her legs. Why do you ask?'

'It would be awful if she were tiny. My eyesight's not that brilliant, and I wouldn't want to miss anything.'

'I'm sure you wouldn't.'

It seemed that Leah's parental home continued to fascinate Gavin, because he asked, 'Is everyone in your hometown so colourful?'

'I doubt it, but I've never really thought about it.' She thought for a moment, and said, 'There are my godparents Bailey and Elaine, although they don't live in Easingthorpe. You'd have to meet Bailey to get the full picture, but he lives in the nineteen-thirties. He's a kind of Wodehousian character, full of charm and bullshit but absolutely delightful. He and my dad did the five-hundred-mile hike together from Poland.'

'Hell's bells.'

'Yes, my mum brought my dad home, and my dad supported Bailey with some help from an American who'd joined the party.'

'No wonder they're all characters.'

'Yes.' She gave him a straight look and said, 'So now you know all about my family. Fair exchange. Let's hear about yours.'

'I haven't got much family.'

'In that case, it won't take long for you to tell me about them.'

'I suppose not. My brother – he's the clever one – is doing a PhD in something to do with French literature, and my dad did a bunk some time ago.'

'Did he die?'

'Not as far as I know. He just sloped off with another woman and left us to fend for ourselves.'

She put a sympathetic hand on his forearm. 'That's awful,' she said.

'It's my mum I feel sorry for. She's rather like Frank's mum, you know, brilliant in adversity, although my mum has one asset that seems to have eluded Mrs Morrison.'

'Go on.'

'There's a bloke who stays with us when he's not away on business. We've called him "Uncle Stan" ever since we were kids, and he's always been good to us all. Graham and I didn't know all that much about him at first and, to be honest, we rather enjoyed the mystery.'

'Fascinating.'

'It has to be said, as well, that Graham would never have gone to university, and I wouldn't have gone to the College without Uncle Stan's help. He's a good bloke.'

Conversation was suspended as the waitress arrived with Leah's chicken salad and Gavin's bangers and mash. Gleefully, he pointed to the dish of peas and carrots that accompanied it.'

'Okay,' said Leah, 'that looks healthy enough.'

12

Leah picked up a programme and took it to her seat. According to Gavin, the items were all 'pot boilers', meaning that they were standard repertoire, but they would be no worse for that. It had to be remembered that it would be the first time some of the students would hear them, and the lunch-time recitals were for their benefit, after all. As she scanned the items, she realised that it would also be her first time, which wasn't really surprising, as her knowledge of the piano repertoire was extremely limited.

The first item was *Scherzo Op 31, no. 2 in B flat minor* by F. Chopin. It would be followed by *Barcarolle Op 60 in F sharp* by F. Chopin. As far as she knew, the *barcarolle* was associated with Venetian gondolas, so that would be interesting. The final piece would be *Paganini Study no. 6* by F. Liszt.

At one-fifteen, Gavin entered the recital hall, stepped on to the platform and bowed discreetly before taking his seat at the piano.

The *Scherzo* provided entertainment from its whimsical beginning to its dramatic and climactic end, and Leah was delighted to see that Gavin's body movements throughout were restricted to those that were apparently necessary. Judging by their applause, the audience were also delighted. It was very exciting.

The *Barcarolle* provided a distinct contrast with the *Scherzo*, beginning as it did with a gentle but insistent figure in the left hand, supporting a haunting, melodic theme in the right. The whole piece, occupying, Leah imagined, about ten minutes, was a gradual and inevitable build-up to a grand climax that created a feeling of breathlessness, at least as far as she was concerned. Again, the student audience showed its willing appreciation.

The Paganini Study turned out to be a piano arrangement of

Paganini's 24th Caprice, which she had heard at some time. It was a series of variations. She was aware that the word 'variation' had a different meaning in music from the one to which she'd become accustomed in ballet, and this set of variations culminated in a towering and powerful *finale*.

Gavin bowed to the audience, glanced at his watch and waited for the applause to die down. When it did, he said, 'Thank you very much indeed. We have a little time in hand, so I should like to play another of Liszt's Paganini Studies. It's called *La Campanella*, and it means "The Little Bell". This is the little bell.' He sounded a high note on the piano. 'Now you'll recognise it when you hear it.'

He took his seat again to play something that looked and sounded quite impossible. The little bell could be heard performing some very skilful acrobatics, but so could the thundering chords that contrasted with it and brought the piece to its dramatic close.

The eager applause continued for maybe a minute or slightly more, but it still seemed a long time, and Gavin could only shrug and look at his watch in mute apology. The afternoon session had to commence at 2:00.

Leah met him outside after the crowd of admiring students had dispersed. 'Congratulations,' she said. 'I really enjoyed it, and you kept your promise.'

He looked puzzled. 'What promise was that?'

'To show the students that it was possible to play and sit still at the same time. You made no excess *ports de bras*, and your facial expression would have been an asset at any poker game.'

'It's the biggest wonder. I nearly didn't get here this morning.'

'What happened?'

'That bloody car of mine again.'

'Oh? Is it gaining a reputation?'

'You could say that. The heater hose burst and sprayed water all over the electrics. I'll have to grasp the nettle and find something newer.'

'Ah,' said Leah, looking like someone who has the perfect answer. 'If you like, I'll speak to my godfather. He's Sales Director at Blackwell Brothers in Northallerton and he's adept at finding bargains for friends.'

'But I'm not a friend of his.'

'Not yet,' she agreed, 'but tell me what your car is, what you fancy and how much you can afford, and then leave it with me.'

When Gavin had a moment to spare, he phoned the number Leah had given him, gave his name and asked if he might speak with Mr Bailey. It struck him as odd that a director of a firm with a Rover franchise would be prepared to involve himself in the sale of a second-hand runabout, but Leah had insisted that he was the man to contact.

A voice said, 'Bailey speaking. Good afternoon, Mr Lowe. My lovely goddaughter tells me you want to change cars.'

'That's right, Mr Bailey, but I'm afraid I'm looking at the modest end of the market. I don't want to waste your time.'

'My dear old thing, you mustn't worry about that. Leah has given me all the information I need and, as it happens, I can lay my hands on a very nice 'L' registered, fifteen-hundred cc Hillman Avenger. It's done twelve thousand miles – hardly been out of the bally garage – and it's spotless. The colour is "spice metallic". That's brown to you and me. If you're interested, I could have it here for you to see, by Saturday morning.'

It sounded too good to be true. 'I make that three years old, Mr Bailey. Surely that's beyond my pocket.'

'Your trade-in plus three hundred. That's what Leah told me. That's with six months' tax, by the way.'

'Really? That's excellent, Mr Bailey.'

'Happy to help, old chap, and it's just "Bailey", by the way, not "Mr".'

'Very well, er, Bailey. What time should I come on Saturday?'

'Oh, make it ten-thirty. There's no point in leaping out of bed at cock-a-doodle-do just for the sake of it.'

'Right, I'll be there at ten-thirty. Goodbye, er, Bailey.'

'My dear old soul, I'm looking forward to it already. Take care.'

Leah decided to accompany him to Blackwell Brothers, so he called for her at the cottage she rented on Ripley Road.

'I see what you meant about Bailey,' he said. 'He belongs to another age.'

'That's why I said you had to meet him to get the full picture. Once encountered, never forgotten, but he's as honest as the day is long, and he'll do you a good deal. He's been doing it for my mum and dad, and me as well, since he got the job at Blackwell Brothers.'

'When was that?' He was finding the history of the Hinchcliffe family somehow compelling, and it seemed necessary to know those things.

'Shortly before I was born, I believe. That was nineteen-fifty-one, so about nineteen-fifty, I'd say.' She added, 'I'm hopeless with numbers, so don't quote me.'

He changed down to join the A1, de-clutching and revving in neutral.

Leah asked, 'Why do you do that?'

'What, double de-clutch? It just makes gear changing so much easier with this excuse for a gearbox.'

She patted the fascia soothingly. 'He doesn't mean it,' she said. 'Please don't break down now.'

'Do you find it helps,' he asked, 'talking to cars?'

'Of course. I talk to mine all the time, and he responds with good behaviour.'

'I thought cars were female.'

'Only when they belong to men.'

They drove on in silence, until Gavin said, 'Tell me more about Bailey. He fascinates me.'

'Okay. He and my dad were PoWs together in Poland. They walked five-hundred-and-fifty miles to a place in Germany, where they were liberated, and Bailey maintains that he'd have died of starvation and exhaustion if it hadn't been for my dad. Anyway, they met again, as I told you, shortly before I was born, and they've lived in each other's pockets ever since. He met his wife Elaine when they were in my dad's first show – she's lovely, by the way – and they got married not long afterwards.'

'I believe you said something about a daughter with a problem.'

'Oh yes, Janice. She has Down's syndrome.' She looked at him, suspecting she might be speaking a foreign language, and said, 'Flat features, almond-shaped eyes and retarded learning.'

'I know what you mean. I'd never heard it called that.' He was quiet for a while, and then he said, 'It must have been an awful shock for them, I mean, when she was born.'

'I've no doubt it was, but they're brilliant with her, and Janice is a lovely girl when she feels secure and she knows what's going on. If something goes wrong for her, though, she can't manage her frustration, and that's when she's difficult.'

They went on in silence, until they came to Leeming.

'The road's signed to Northallerton,' said Leah. 'It's a right turn when we get to it.'

'Is everything "right" and "left" when you navigate?'

'Mm, it's the easiest way. I can't get the hang of "third exit" and that sort of thing. I find that roundabouts grow extra exits when I'm not looking, and I get confused.'

They approached the roundabout, where the road to Northallerton was clearly signed.

'There,' said Leah when they were on the A684, 'you'd have been lost without me.'

'Completely bewildered,' he agreed.

'My dad says that maps might be written in Arabic for all the use they are to me. Mind you, with his sense of direction, he has no room to talk. My mum's the navigator in our family.'

'Well, you haven't let me down yet.' Mention of her father set a process of thought in motion, because he asked, 'How did your parents meet?'

'My mum wrote letters to my dad and sent him parcels when he was a PoW. They got to know each other incredibly well, and then he wrote her a song.' She broke off to say, 'My dad writes songs the way other people pass comments. You know what I mean, because you're the same. Anyway, this particular song was about how she made everything better for him, and he ended it by telling her he loved her. She was thrilled to bits, because she felt the same way about him.'

'And they'd never met?'

'No, they met eventually in Trafalgar Square, and it was hearts and flowers from then on. Lovely, isn't it?'

'It certainly is. From your descriptions, I almost know your family.'

Suddenly, she was aware of an omission. 'I haven't told you about Rhea,' she said.

'Who's Rhea?'

'She's a music-loving Aberdeen Terrier who arranges plant pots in ever-changing patterns.'

'I'd expect nothing less than that from a cultured animal like a Scottie.'

She looked at him in surprise. 'Do you know the breed?'

'I grew up with one next door. I used to take him for walks, and I talked to him the way you talk to your car. He was a great listener.'

'I talk to animals as well. By the way, go straight on at the junction, and then the showroom is about five hundred yards on your left.'

He negotiated the junction and drove on for about half a mile before spotting the showroom. 'That was a funny five hundred yards,' he said.

'I told you I was hopeless with numbers.'

'Anyway,' he said, turning on to the forecourt, 'here we are.' It was ten-fifteen.

They left the car and entered the showroom, where a young and eager assistant asked if he could help them.

'We've come to see Bailey,' said Leah, 'but we're a touch early. The appointment's at ten-thirty.'

'I'll see if he's available.' The young man left the showroom, returning after a brief interval to say, 'He'll be with you shortly. Please take a seat. Can I offer you coffee or tea?'

'Yes, please. Coffee would be nice, wouldn't it Gavin?'

Her question went unheeded, as Gavin was no longer by her side. He was examining a brown metallic Hillman Avenger parked on the forecourt.

'Just coffee for me, then, please.'

'Certainly, madam.'

Being called 'madam' was a new experience for Leah, and she

was trying to decide whether she enjoyed it or resented being taken for a matron, when Bailey appeared, looking immaculate in a dove-grey three-piece suit.

'My darling girl,' he said, 'suddenly my morning is brighter.' He kissed the proffered cheek and asked, 'Where is your friend?'

Leah pointed to the forecourt, where Gavin was still inspecting the Avenger. 'It's a whole, new relationship,' she said.

'Let's go and join him.'

They left the showroom to walk the short distance to the car and its rapt admirer.

'Bailey,' said Leah, 'this is Gavin. Gavin, meet the infamous Bailey.'

'Mr Lowe.' Bailey extended his hand.

'I prefer "Gavin".' It seemed right to dispense with titles altogether.

'Gavin, this, as you've probably gathered, is the car I told you about. Would you like to take it for a spin?' He produced the key from his pocket.

'Yes, please. Are you coming, Leah?'

'No, I want to have a word with Bailey. You go and enjoy yourself.' She returned to the showroom with Bailey to find that her coffee was still drinkable. As she sat down, Bailey said, 'I must thank you for mending Janice's radio.'

'It was nothing, Bailey. The battery had become half disconnected, that's all.'

'Well, you know I'm just about practical enough to open a phone book and call an electrician.'

'There's no need now. Janice had tried to mend it by smashing it against the wall, and I could see she was getting into a state about it. Luckily, it was something simple.'

'Bless you, Leah. What did you want to speak to me about?' He glanced at Leah's cup, saw that it was half-full, and poured one for himself.

'Martin, basically. I've tried talking to Mum and Dad, but they're both too close to the problem to see it clearly.'

'Do you mean about his shyness?'

'Yes, it's almost as if he cuts himself off deliberately. I thought

I'd play Cupid and get him fixed up with the girl across the road. I know he's interested in her and I thought she'd do him a power of good. For one thing, she'd do all his talking for him, but when I suggested it, he told me to forget it.'

Bailey sipped his coffee and grimaced. 'Is that the girl in last year's show, who lives across the way from the Hinchcliffe residence? The one who never closes her bedroom curtains?'

Leah let her eyelids fall shut. 'So you've noticed her as well.'

'It was quite by chance.' He looked thoughtful and said, 'Any approach would need to come from Martin, but if he told you to forget it, that's what you must do. Some people who suffer from shyness learn to control it to some extent, but you'll never cure it, and he would resent being pitchforked into a relationship, however casual.' He smiled sympathetically. 'My advice, Leah, for what it's worth, is to let sleeping dogs lie.'

'Like you, Bailey, your advice is priceless. Thank you.'

'That's what godfathers are for, dear girl.' He looked through the showroom window as Gavin drove in and parked the car on the forecourt. 'I believe we have a happy customer, Leah. Let's go and talk to him.'

When Bailey and Gavin were satisfied with the arrangements, Bailey gestured to the eager youth to join them.

'This is Andrew,' he said. 'Andrew, I want you to prepare the documents for Mr Lowe according to the notes I've made. There's nothing to negotiate – I've done all that – and put the sale down as yours. You won't get rich on the commission,' he said cryptically, 'but I can't take it, I don't need it, and you're more than welcome to it.'

Andrew's eyes opened wide. 'Thanks, Mr Bailey.'

'Think nothing of it, Andrew. Now, Gavin and Leah, I must leave you in Andrew's increasingly capable hands. Keep in touch, Leah.' He kissed her upturned cheek and then offered his hand to Gavin. 'Happy motoring, Gavin.'

'Thank you, Bailey. I'm very grateful.'

It had been a useful morning for Leah and a successful one for Gavin.

Their next event would be the auditions for the show.

13

Gavin suggested, and Neil agreed, that the dancers' auditions would be best left to Leah, who was naturally pleased with the decision. She was invited, also, to attend the acting and singing auditions on the basis that four opinions were better than three. The panel that met in the dance studio, therefore, comprised Vincent, Neil, Gavin and Leah, and the first part to be cast was that of Queen Elizabeth the First.

'Judith Eldridge,' announced Vincent. 'Judith, would you like to read the extract from the script?'

'Okay, Vincent.' Judith struck a haughty pose and read, ' "For four hundred years I've been remembered as a virgin, and I've had to live up to my reputation. Well, I've had enough. I want a man." '

'Judith love,' said Neil, 'do you really think she had an American accent? I mean, they named a colony after her, fair enough, but that was four thousand miles away.'

'Well, what sort of accent would she have, then?'

'English upper class, if you can manage it. Go again, darling.'

'Okay. "For four hundred years ai've been remembered as a virgin, and ai've had to live up to mai reputation—'

'Judith,' said Vincent. 'Would you like to sing for us?'

'Okay.' The tenacious student launched herself into 'The Way we Were,' until Gavin said in what he hoped was a kindly tone. 'That's okay, Judith, thank you.'

'Thank you, Judith,' said Vincent.

'Don't you want me to read again?'

'No, that won't be necessary.'

Suddenly, her expression brightened. 'Have I got the part, then?'

'We'll let you know.'

They heard four more students before they were able to cast 'QE One', as Neil insisted on calling the distinguished monarch.

The next part to be cast was that of Queen Mary Tudor.

'There's only one student auditioning for this part,' said Neil, opening the studio door. 'Lynne Stevenson,' he announced.

Lynne, a second-year student, walked confidently into the studio.

Neil asked, 'you know the character, don't you, love? She's called "Bloody Mary".'

'That's funny,' said Lynne. 'I thought she was in *South Pacific*.'

'She got around quite a lot,' Neil told her. 'Between you and me, I think she had a bike.'

'Kidding.' Lynne gave him a cheeky look as she took the script from him. Then, having read through it, she declared herself ready.

' "Again, this child, this wilful opportunist, dares to challenge me, and that after four hundred years! I will not have it! I will see her....' Lynne looked meaningfully downwards. 'I will see her *elsewhere* first. Those are my final words!' She looked to the panel and asked, 'Are they really her final words, or does she get to sing?'

'It's a singing part,' Gavin reminded her. 'I see you've brought something.'

'Yes, although I don't know how appropriate it is, not knowing the music for the part.'

'It's not yet written,' said Gavin. 'What have you brought to sing?'

' "Just You Wait, Henry Higgins" from *My Fair Lady*.'

'It's a good choice.' Gavin took the score from her and went to the piano.

After a convincing performance of the song, Vincent said, 'Thank you, Lynne. We'll let you know.'

Lynne took back her score and then hesitated. 'Sorry about the "Bloody Mary" thing,' she said. 'I tend to make jokes when I'm nervous.'

'It's not a bad way to manage nerves,' Vincent told her, 'and there's no harm done.'

Lynne left the studio to general agreement that she was as good a Mary Tudor as they were likely to find. He went on to announce

Queen Cleopatra, and the first student to audition for the part, Debbie Ghyll.' He asked Miss Ghyll to step inside.

Debbie shimmied in with an air of total confidence.

'Now, Debbie,' said Vincent, 'there's not a lot of script with this part, but we'd like you to read this.' He handed her the prepared extract, which she read to herself.

'Okay?'

'Okay,' she confirmed. Then striking a proprietorial pose, she read, ' "Is my asses' milk ready? And my honey? I feel a bath coming on." ' This was one part that needed an American accent, and Debbie's accent and vocal mannerisms were vintage Mae West. ' "Hey, make with the asses' milk, can't you? I wanna *immerse* myself." '

'Thank you, Debbie darling,' said Neil. 'Have you something you'd like to sing for us?'

'Yes, I've got the dots here, if Gavin wouldn't mind playing.'

'By all means.' Gavin took the sheet music from her. It was 'I'm in the Mood for Love', and it seemed a natural choice, given the part and Debbie's chosen persona.

They listened to the end, when, just as Neil was about to speak, Vincent said, 'Thank you very much, Debbie. We'll let you know.'

Debbie left the studio, and Vincent whispered something to Neil before addressing the others. 'Well, I think Cleopatra was reborn, just now, as Mae West. What do you think?'

'She gets my vote,' said Gavin.

'And mine.' Leah was equally convinced.

'Is anyone at all interested in what I think?'

'Oh, for goodness' sake, Neil,' said Vincent, 'of course we are.'

'Well, I was about to congratulate Debbie on her performance, when you interrupted me. I mean, I'm only the bloody director here, as well as the author, or haven't you noticed?'

'You know why I interrupted you, Neil. Now, shall we get on with these auditions?'

'Oh, all-bloody-right.'

For the sake of fairness, they listened to three more Cleopatras, none of whom could compete with Debbie Ghyll.

Vincent asked, 'What's next, Neil?'

'King Philip the Second of Spain.' A note of asperity still lingered in Neil's tone. Leah turned to Gavin and winked, pushing out her lower lip and making it tremble.

Vincent opened the door to ask, 'Who's going first for King Philip of Spain?'

A voice answered, 'Angus McLeod.'

'Come in, Angus, and read this for us, if you will.' Vincent gave him the audition extract.

Gavin knew Angus. He was a singing student from Edinburgh, and it would be interesting to see how he coped with the accent.

Angus studied the script and pronounced himself ready. Assuming a haughty manner, he read in a pleasingly convincing Spanish accent, ' "I am to be banished to the Underworld, and why? It is simply because I fail to see anything wrong in torturing a few English sailors and other heretics. What is the Hereafter coming to if the innocent and enthralling practice of human torment is seen as something less than acceptable?" '

'Thank you, Angus,' said Vincent. 'What are you going to sing for us?'

' "You've Got to Pick a Pocket or Two", if that's all right.'

Gavin took the score from him and placed it on the piano. 'It's a good choice,' he said.

The panel listened to a very able portrayal of Fagin. At the end, Vincent was obliged to tell Angus that they would let him know, even though they were already convinced by his audition.

The next student was Nigel Thackeray, also for King Philip of Spain. He took the extract with a flourish and read, ' "I am to be banished to the Underworld, and—" '

'Nigel,' said Neil, 'Can you do it more as a Spanish potentate and less like Jacques in *As You Like It*?'

'Sorry, Neil love, I'll go again.' He tried once more.

'Nigel, that was like Ken Barlow in *Coronation Street*.'

'Neil love, I need time to prepare. This is too immediate, like a slap in the face.'

'Try again, Nigel,' said Vincent. 'Think grandiose and outraged.'

Nigel made a third attempt, which was now closer to Larry Grayson.

Neil asked, 'What would you like to sing for us, Nigel?'

' "I Can See Clearly Now".'

'Have you brought any dots?'

'Gavin love, I can't be expected to think of everything.' He went on to sing his song reasonably well, but his reading had already ruled him out. Vincent wasn't yet finished with him, however.

'Nigel,' he said, 'this has nothing to do with your audition, but I must point out that you've addressed two members of the academic staff as "love", and I don't want to hear that again. Do you hear me?'

'All right, Vincent. I'll go, then, shall I?'

'Yes, Nigel, we'll let you know.'

Next on the agenda was King Henry the Seventh, and the first to audition for it was Kevin Good, who scanned the script and began.

' "My reign on Earth was tenuous. In the 'Ereafter all things are eternal—"'

'Kevin,' said Neil, 'I don't think he would have spoken in broad Yorkshire. In any case, he was a descendant of the House of Lancaster.'

'I don't think I can do a Lancashire accent, Neil.'

'Neither would he, love. He was a king, not a bloody road sweeper.'

Vincent looked over his glasses at Neil, who shrugged and went on to say, 'Go again, Kevin, and try to make him a bit regal, for good-ness' sake.'

' "My reign on Hearth was tenuous: hin the 'Earafter all things are heternal...." ' He continued to the end.

'Thank you, Kevin. What are you going to sing for us?'

' "Take Me Home Country Roads".'

'Any dots?'

'No, I couldn't find t' music this morning.'

When he had sung and departed, 'Neil said, 'That was supposed to be about going home to West Virginia, but it sounded more like 'Uddersfield, 'Alifax and all stations east.'

'It's a shame,' said Leah. 'He's an excellent tap dancer.'

'Maybe we can use him for that. Anyway, who's next?'

Vincent went to the door and enquired. 'Stephen Price,' he re-ported. 'Come in, Stephen.'

Stephen came into the studio wearing a black cloak and carrying a music score, which he gave to Gavin. 'Would you mind playing, Gavin? When we get to it, it's "Happy Feet".' He took the script and, as he took his place, it was evident that he was wearing tap shoes. He read the script to himself. 'Right,' he said, 'I'm ready.'

'Okay,' said Neil.

Stephen gathered the cloak about him and read in a deep, sepulchral tone, ' "My reign on Earth was tenuous. In the Hereafter, all things are eternal. Which is the better? A contested throne or to dwell among the lesser members of one's calling, where the only relief from tedium is...." ' Loosening the strings of his cloak, he cast it aside, saying, ' "Music, merriment and dancing!" '

Gavin began 'Happy Feet', and Stephen was immediately in his chosen sphere, singing the song with evident enjoyment, until the middle eight bars, when he broke into a tap routine, which he executed with skill.

At the end of the number, Vincent said, 'Thank you, Stephen. We'll certainly let you know.'

The panel was unanimous that Stephen should be given the part. It was a bright and positive end to the first session.

Afterwards, Gavin said, 'I wonder what Vincent said to Neil that put him in such a petulant mood.'

'I overheard him,' said Leah. 'He was telling him to go easy on the "loves" and "darlings" when he addresses the students. It's not before time, if you ask me.'

'You need an antidote, I can tell.'

'What do you have in mind?'

He looked at his watch. It was six-thirty-five. 'Do you fancy a drink before we go home?'

Her expression softened. 'Why not? The Duke's Head?'

They walked up the road to the pub, where Leah found a table while Gavin went to the bar, returning with a glass of dry white wine and a glass of red.

He asked, 'What are you cooking tonight?'

'Why? Are you thinking of gate-crashing?'

'Nothing so presumptuous. I wondered if you'd like to eat here and save yourself the trouble.'

'Okay, let's have a look at the menu.' She gave him an inquisitive look and said, 'That was a snap decision of yours, to eat here.'

'Not really. There's no food in the flat. I'll have to go shopping tomorrow. In any case, I can't find my can opener.'

'I'm happy to join you here, but are you afraid to eat alone?'

'Not afraid. Let's just say it's one of those things best done by two or more.'

'You're probably right. Is that why you're on wine rather than beer?'

'Yes.'

'I thought so.' She put the menu down, and said, 'The chicken Kiev beckons.'

'So does the steak-and-kidney pie.' He went to the bar to order.

Returning to the table, he said, 'Neil really is your bugbear, isn't he?'

'I prefer to call him my *bête noire*, because it sounds more appropriate for a pretentious wally like him. There's all the difference in the world between Bailey's posing and Neil's sickening act. For one thing, Bailey is a genuine human being.'

'And Neil's not?'

'No, he's not. I resent the way he treated my rejection of him, telling you among others that I was a lesbian.'

Gavin looked uncomfortable. 'I still feel bad about that,' he said.

'You weren't to know. They don't all wear dungarees and look like Charles Bronson.' She gave him a mischievous look and said, 'Besides, when you first arrived, I wondered for a while if you might be gay.'

Startled, Gavin put his glass down, and asked, 'What on earth gave you that idea?'

She laughed. 'The boot's on the other foot now, isn't it?'

'No, tell me.'

'Poor old Gavin.' She was still laughing. 'It was because you were so nice,' she told him. 'When we met outside Vincent's office, you offered to get me a chair because I was on crutches, and then, when we went inside, you moved the coffee table for me. You also picked up my briefcase when I dropped it.'

'If you think it's necessary to be gay in order to be civilised, you must have known a lot of cavemen.'

'I've known a few out-and-out bastards,' she confirmed.

'I'm sorry to hear that.'

'Discounting family and friends, I haven't a very high opinion of the male sex. There's a few – you, Vincent and one or two others I regard as exceptions – but, in general, that's where I stand.'

'You know,' he said, wondering quite how to respond to such a dramatic disclosure, 'I'm not even going to try to apologise for my fellow travellers.'

'Don't,' she advised. 'Just go on being one of the exceptions.'

'It's the only role I know.' Then, changing the subject, he asked, 'What are people wearing for the ruby wedding, by the way?'

'I'm glad you asked, because it had slipped my mind to tell you. It's formal. Black tie, as far as you're concerned.'

'Overalls, eh?' A disquieting thought occurred to him, and he asked, 'Do you think I'm ready for the dance floor?'

'There'll be those less accomplished than you,' she assured him, 'and some won't have a clue. In any case, you'll only dance with me, and probably my mum, and neither of us is going to bite you if you go wrong.'

When it came, the food was good, and the conversation was easy. Eventually, however, it was time to leave. As they stepped on to the pavement, Gavin offered her his arm.

She said, 'You keep doing it, don't you?'

'What?'

'Being nice.'

'It's to save your knee.'

'And I appreciate it.'

They reached the carpark and Gavin walked her to her car.

'Thank you,' she said. 'I'm not keen on this carpark after dark.' She found her key and unlocked the car. 'I'll pay next time. That was sneaky, paying when you ordered the food. Anyway, thank you for a lovely meal.' She inclined her head for him to kiss her cheek.

14

'Leah, you look fantastic.' Her gown was in a summery, floral pattern with a halter neck. Gavin had never seen her in anything other than jeans, and the effect was particularly pleasing.

'Thank you, Gavin. I do my best.' She took down her coat, and he helped her on with it. He waited while she locked the door and put the key in her bag, and then offered her his arm.

'That's a lovely, old-fashioned thing to do,' she said. 'It's still a novelty.'

'It's all part of my musical upbringing.'

'Your clarinet teacher did a great job.'

He unlocked the passenger door and opened it, holding it until she'd gathered her skirt and was safely in her seat.

'This car is superb after the old Morris,' he said, starting the engine.

'You're in love. I can tell.'

'Oh, you can mock, but you don't know how frustrating life used to be.'

'Possibly not. Do you know the way to the Cricket Club, by the way?'

'Yes, I drove round that way yesterday, after work.'

'You flew over it, did you? That's another of my dad's expressions. He always has to "fly over" places to fix the directions in his mind before he actually goes there.'

He slowed down to join the main road, and asked, 'Was he a pilot?'

'No, a telegraphist air gunner. He had a go at flying, but he always tried to land the aeroplane when it was still twenty feet in the air. They said aeroplanes were too precious to be wasted on him, so they gave him a radio and a machine-gun instead.' She smiled at the thought. 'I can't imagine my dad with a machine-gun.'

'Not his kind of thing?'

'Not in the slightest. He's a gentle soul.'

'Tell me,' he said, changing the subject, 'do the people who are hosting the party live near your parents?'

'No, they did, but they sold their place and retired to Harrogate quite recently. I think Mr Cresswell's health might have had something to do with it.'

'Oh, is he in a bad way?' It seemed odd that he was hosting a lavish party.

'Not really; at least, as far as I know, but farming is for the fit and active, and he's no longer young. He's certainly older than she is. You'll see when we get there.'

They turned off the main road and continued for two miles until they came to Stackgarth Lane, which led to Nidderdale Cricket, Bowling and Athletics Club.

'It looks like a substantial place,' he observed.

'It is. It's all the things it's called, as well as being a kind of country club. It's a local landmark that's been there for ever.' She corrected herself by saying, 'Well, since before I was born, anyway.'

'Oh, that's going some.'

'Don't be foul. I bet you're older than I am.'

'I'm twenty-seven.'

'There, then. I'm only twenty-four.'

'A mere child,' he agreed, turning into the wide gateway and drive that led to the carpark.

Having left their coats in the cloakroom, they went through to the ballroom, where a number of guests were already seated at the tables around the perimeter. Leah waved to two people she recognised, and led Gavin towards a mature couple whom he imagined correctly to be the host and hostess.

'Mr and Mrs Cresswell,' said Leah, 'congratulations on making it to forty, not out, and thank you for the invitation. I've been looking forward to this.'

They exchanged pleasantries, and Leah said, 'I'd like to introduce my friend and colleague Gavin Lowe.'

With that formality discharged, she took him to meet the couple she'd recognised on the way in.

'Hello, Mum. Hello, Dad. She greeted her parents and said, 'This is Gavin. He plays dance music on the clarinet.'

'And alto sax,' added Gavin. 'How d' you do? I'm delighted to meet you both.'

'Let me get you people a drink,' said Leah's dad.

'Vodka and tonic, please,' said Leah. 'I'm not driving tonight.'

'Thank you, Mr Hinchcliffe. Just a bitter lemon, please. I *am* driving.'

'Bailey fixed him up with a new car,' Leah told them, 'and he's madly in love with it.'

'What have you got?'

'An Avenger.'

'Same as mine,' said Mr Hinchcliffe. 'Good choice.' He headed for the bar.

'It's lovely to meet you, Gavin,' said Mrs Hinchcliffe. 'Leah's told us about the music you're writing for the show, and we're looking forward to hearing it. It seems you and my husband have a lot in common.'

'I could probably benefit from his advice, Mrs Hinchcliffe, 'and I'd certainly value it.'

She laughed shortly. 'You'll probably get it whether you ask for it or not,' she said. She was wearing a blue, tiered gown that, to his untutored eye, was somehow Grecian, and it hung remarkably well on her *petite* figure. As well as that, she had the kind of face that encouraged conversation, because she seemed so transparently pleasant. He recalled Leah's description of her, and it seemed to fall into place.

'I'm looking forward to hearing the band,' he said.

'I've been giving Gavin a crash course in ballroom dancing,' Leah told her. He came here tonight to hear the band, but I told him he has to dance as well.'

'I hope Leah hasn't been too demanding, Gavin,' said Mrs Hinchcliffe. 'She sets very high standards.'

'Of course I do. I'll let you dance with him later, and you can give him an independent assessment.'

'Don't terrify the poor man.' She looked over Leah's shoulder and said, 'Here comes your dad with the drinks.'

His arrival coincided with a stentorian announcement by Mr Cresswell.

'Friends, let me welcome you all here and invite you to help yourselves to food at the buffet.'

As the catering staff removed the covers from the buffet tables, Mr Hinchcliffe said, 'You two go ahead. Mum and I'll sit here and work up an appetite.'

Leah and Gavin each took a plate, and were choosing from a tempting spread of buffet food, when someone said, 'Na'then, Leah, how's the knee?'

Leah turned and smiled. 'Hello, George. It's much better, thank you. How are you keeping?'

'Oh, fair to bloody awful, you know.'

'Gavin, meet George Clay, First Reed with "The Dalesmen". Gavin plays clarinet and sax, George.'

'Gerraway? Maybe you should be playing with us tonight.'

Gavin smiled at the friendly gesture. 'No,' he said, 'I've come to listen.'

'Aye well, I hope you enjoy it.' He moved to the next table and its seductive arrangement of pieces of Scotch egg, pork pie and sausage roll.

Leah and Gavin returned to their table.

'I haven't had much conversation with your dad yet,' said Gavin, as Leah's parents headed for the buffet, 'but your mum's lovely.'

'Yes, what you see is what you get.'

'Is that another of your dad's sayings?'

'No, my brother's, when he makes the effort to converse. He works in the computer industry, and they have a language of their own.'

'I heard your dad call your mum "SP". Are those her initials?'

'No, her name's Sylvia, but "SP" stands for "Sugar Plum", the fairy in *The Nutcracker*. It's his personal nickname for her.'

'They seem to have a great relationship.'

Leah nodded, and said wistfully, 'I wish I knew the secret.'

'You're joking, surely?'

'You wouldn't think that if you knew my history.'

As Mr and Mrs Hinchcliffe returned from the buffet, Gavin stood and waited until they were seated before sitting again. His gesture drew an approving look from Leah's mum.

'Have you been waiting for us?' Mr Hinchcliffe's question seemed to be born of disbelief. 'It won't do you any good on the plate, you know.'

'Gavin's a gentleman,' explained Leah, 'and I'm enjoying the novelty; in fact, I'm thinking of having him preserved.'

'Leah,' said her mum gently, 'you'll embarrass the poor man.'

To change the subject, Gavin asked, 'How's the pantomime coming along, Mr Hinchcliffe?'

'Call me "Freddy". Everybody else does. It's the usual thing with just two months to go, but they'll get there.' He smiled. 'Sylvia's been drilling the chorus of children, trying to make them look like sailors.'

Mrs Hinchcliffe grimaced. 'I always hated squad drill when I was in the Wrens, but I'm beginning to understand how our instructors must have felt.'

'Poor little buggers,' said Freddy with feeling, 'being put through their paces by Leading Wren Charlesworth.'

'I'm sure you do it in the kindest way, Mrs Hinchcliffe.'

' "Sylvia",' she corrected him. 'It's only "SP" that's exclusive to Freddy.'

'So I understand.' He decided it was time to reveal his ignorance. 'It's a long time since I saw a pantomime,' he said, 'and I'm wondering what sailors have to do with Dick Whittington.'

'If you remember,' explained Sylvia, 'a sum of money goes missing at the home of Alderman Fitzwarren, and Dick is suspected, so he goes on a sea voyage to Morocco, where he makes his fortune.'

'So that's how it's done,' said Freddy. 'I might be tempted to give it a try, but the last time I flew over the Med, I found myself swimming in it.'

'What kind of aircraft was it, Freddy?'

'A Fairey Albacore. Do you know the type?'

'I made a model of one years ago,' admitted Gavin a little self-consciously. 'I made a Swordfish as well.'

'They were a damned sight better than the Albacore. At least, they had an engine that could be trusted to keep going.'

'But,' said Sylvia, 'if you hadn't had to ditch, you wouldn't have been taken prisoner and you wouldn't have met me.'

Quite unnecessarily, Leah took over the baton. 'And I would never have been born, and you would have been at home this evening, Gavin, glueing model aeroplanes together.'

'You mustn't make fun, Leah.'

'It's all right, Sylvia,' said Gavin. 'I have a thick skin.'

Someone cleared his throat in front of a microphone.

'David Cresswell,' said, Leah, 'the son.'

'Good evening everyone. I hope you're all enjoying the buffet. I'd just like to say a few words on this special occasion.' He went on to make a mercifully short speech about his parents, including a few 'in' jokes that provoked polite laughter. Finally, he proposed a toast to the couple, announcing that dancing would follow. Gavin looked around, but Freddy had disappeared. As if by an elaborate illusion, the band had also appeared on the platform.

Freddy appeared and, suddenly, they were playing 'Zip-a-Dee-Doo-Dah' from *Song of the South*. Then, Freddy went to the microphone and welcomed everyone on behalf of the band. 'Let's begin with a waltz,' he suggested. 'Let's have "By the Sleepy Lagoon".'

'Come on, Gavin.' Leah took his hand to tow him on to the floor. 'What do you think of the band?'

'They're great.' It was the briefest of accolades because Gavin had to concentrate on getting everything right, partly because Leah expected it, but also because he didn't want to look awkward in front of Sylvia.

'Rise and fall,' Leah reminded him gently.'

Gavin led, concentrating as hard as he could, but still with an ear for the music, that he remembered as the theme for a radio programme his mother used to listen to regularly, called *Desert Island Discs*.

The number ended, with Gavin relieved on the one hand, that he'd survived it without going horribly wrong, but also feeling that he would have liked it to continue for a little longer, now he'd got the hang of the waltz.

'Thank you.' He joined her in applauding the band, and they re-joined Sylvia.

The next number was 'When I Fall in Love', a foxtrot.

Leah sat back in her chair and said, 'Are you going to ask Mum to dance, Gavin? You can do this one.'

Gavin took a deep breath and, sounding more confident than he felt, asked, 'Would you like to dance, Sylvia?'

'I'd love to.' She took his hand and allowed him to lead her on to the floor. 'You're not on trial,' she reminded him. 'We're all here to enjoy ourselves. Nothing more than that.'

'This is the hard one,' he admitted.

'Just go with the music, and I'll go wherever you go.'

She was as good as her word, following him like a shadow. Eventually, she said, 'Leah's taught you well, but there's one thing she's forgotten to tell you.'

'What's that?' He wasn't aware he'd gone wrong.

'Nothing technical, but it seems she hasn't told you to enjoy it. Relax, Gavin.'

He relaxed as far as he was able, so that by the end of the number he was actually taking pleasure in it.

'Thank you, Sylvia.' He applauded the band and accompanied her back to the table.

'Well done,' said Leah.

'Yes,' agreed Sylvia, 'you've got the idea. All you need now is practice.'

They sat through a cha-cha-cha because it wasn't yet part of Gavin's repertoire, and then Freddy handed over to the pianist before joining them at their table.

Leah whispered, 'They're going to play "Love Walked In". It's a slow foxtrot.'

Gavin asked, 'How do you know what they're going to play?'

'Trust me.'

Desmond, the pianist, came to the microphone to say, 'The next number is a slow foxtrot: "Love Walked In", and here to sing it is Christine.'

Gavin shook his head in bemusement, but took Leah's hand as she propelled him on to the floor.

'As soon as Desmond takes over,' Leah explained, 'they play "Love Walked In". It's one of my mum's favourites to dance to.'

It made perfect sense, and now that he was less anxious, he began to enjoy the soft beat of the number. Also, the singer was very good. Occasionally, he caught sight of Freddy and Sylvia, who smiled briefly before returning to their own romantic microcosm. Leah caught him looking, and said, 'They're still daft about each other, you know.'

'I'm not surprised.'

When they returned to their table, Gavin started to pick up the empty glasses. He asked, 'Is everyone having the same again?'

Leah and Sylvia confirmed that they would, but Freddy said, 'I'm going on to goffers because I'm driving. I'll have the same as you, thanks, Gavin.'

' "Goffers" are soft drinks,' Leah translated helpfully.

Gavin took his place at the bar and was served quickly with a vodka and tonic, a gin and tonic, and two bitter lemons. He was putting them on a tray, when he heard Sylvia's voice close by. She was talking to Mrs Cresswell, and seemed to be answering a question about Leah.

'Her knee is very much better, as you can see. Yes, it's good to see her relaxing and enjoying herself again.'

Mrs Cresswell said something that Gavin didn't quite catch, and then Sylvia said, 'Oh, him. I'm glad to say she's got him out of her system now, although what she saw in him in the first place was a mystery. She seems to attract the worst kind of men.'

Gavin was guiltily aware that he was eavesdropping, but he was unable to make himself move on, until he heard Sylvia say, 'Actually, the young man she's brought tonight couldn't be more different from her usual choice. He seems very nice indeed, and he knows how to behave in company.'

Now beset with guilt, Gavin carried the tray of drinks back to the table.

Freddy asked, 'Have you seen Sylvia, by any chance, Gavin?'

'I saw her by the bar, talking to Mrs Cresswell.'

'Oh, that could be a long job.' He picked up his glass and said, 'Thanks, Gavin. I'll have to go and relieve Desmond, but before I go, I must ask you, are you at all keen on fly fishing?'

Gavin saw Leah close her eyes in desperation, but he pretended not to notice. 'I'm afraid not,' he said.

'Oh well, it's not everybody's passion.' He touched Leah's arm and said, 'Tell your mum I'll be back for "All the Things You Are".'

'Okay, Dad.'

When he was gone, Leah said, 'After my mum, dance music and photography, his passion is fly fishing. My granddad introduced him to it after the war. Ever since then, he's been evangelical about it. Of course, it may just be that he's looking for a fishing partner, but few things get him as excited as a trout on the end of his line.'

'I'm afraid I don't know the first thing about fishing of any kind.'

'Don't worry about it. Neither do I.'

Gavin danced again with Leah and Sylvia. He was enjoying it much more now; in fact, it was entirely possible that it could become the new enthusiasm in his life, and he intimated as much to Leah, who told him she had witnessed similar conversions in her brief experience.

Eventually, Desmond took over the baton, and Freddy re-joined them at the table.

'Take your partners,' said Desmond, 'for the foxtrot of the evening, because the music is none other than the sublime "All the Things You Are", and here again to sing it for us is Christine.'

As Freddy and Sylvia headed for the floor, Gavin asked, 'Is this another regular fixture?'

'You bet. It means a lot to them. Remind me to tell you the story some time, and it's a beautiful song anyway. Are we going to dance?'

'Of course.'

The foxtrot was now almost second nature to him. Also, he recalled playing the song at one time, but this was the first time he'd heard the lyrics.

Leah seemed to sense his new involvement, because she moved closer to him until he was conscious of her perfume, her breath on his cheek, and the feel of her lissom, toned back against his right palm.

He drew up outside her cottage and said, 'Thank you for a very special evening.'

'Thank you, Gavin. I enjoyed it too.'

He switched off the engine. 'Let me walk you to the door,' he said.

'There's no need.'

'It's an uneven path. I feel I owe it to your knee after the sterling service it's performed tonight.'

'Oh, all right, then.'

He opened her car door and helped her out.

'My mum's going to talk about your beautiful manners for weeks on end,' she said.

He thought about her conversation with Mrs Cresswell, and said, 'I'm sure she has other things to talk about.'

As they reached the door of the cottage, she said, 'Normally, I'd invite you in for coffee, but it's very late.'

'Very late,' he agreed. 'It's a quarter to pumpkin time already.'

She leaned forward, offering her cheek, and Gavin gave her a discreet peck, resolved to take one step at a time.

15

"'The going's firm, and everywhere, there's nervous expectation,
All bets are off, the viewers sense the punters' trepidation.'"

Gavin stopped them to say, 'The last syllable of each line is *staccato*. You all know what that means, don't you?'

Heads nodded.

'Good, so let's make them really *staccato*.' He was about to resume, when a chorus member raised his hand.

'Gavin love?'

He summoned his patience. 'Just "Gavin", please.'

'Sorry, Gavin. We spend so much time with Neil, you see.'

'Evidently. What do you want to ask me?'

'Who are these "viewers"?'

'Racing enthusiasts at home. There'll be at least two dummy cameras upstage and overhead. I'm told you can't have a major horse race without TV coverage.'

'I suppose not.'

'Good.'

The chorus resumed, articulating the *staccato* syllables adequately, and the rehearsal seemed to be going well until the student who had asked the question about viewers raised his hand again.

Memories of Kevin McNamara threatened to return. 'What is it, Nigel?'

'It's this line about a sultan coming from behind, Gavin.'

'Yes, it's not a *double entendre*.' He motioned to the chorus to stop laughing. 'He's simply accelerating.'

'I didn't mean that. I'm saying, do we really have sultans in the show?'

'As far as I'm aware, there isn't one in the cast.'

'That's what I thought, so why is there one in this chorus, love?'

Again, Gavin mustered his patience. 'Call it poetic licence, Nigel, and on the subject of licence, you addressed me again as "love". I don't like it, so please don't do it again.'

'All right.'

'Also, if you have any more questions about the lyrics, please save them for the end of the rehearsal. That way, everyone gets a share of my attention.'

'All right.' There was a degree of petulance in the response but, for the sake of the rehearsal, Gavin overlooked it.

By the end of the rehearsal, he was confident that the opening chorus was secure. Nigel had tried once more to interrupt the proceedings, but a warning look had been sufficient to deter him.

'At this point,' Leah told her dancers, 'the chorus will divide and move stage right and left to reveal a waist-high screen painted to resemble railings at a racecourse. That's is when you make your entrance.' She added, 'And your exit. It's a very brief appearance, although you'll do the sequence in slow motion.'

One student asked, 'How will we do that, Leah?'

'That's what you're about to find out.'

Another said, 'I don't get it. Are we supposed to be the jockeys or the horses?'

'Essentially, you're both, but only the jockeys and the horses' heads are visible to the audience.'

The same student appeared to be struggling with the whole concept. She asked, 'What's our costume for this?'

'Racing colours and crowns.'

'Crowns?'

'Crowns. The race is allegorical, a kind of metaphor for the election to the Upper Chambers.'

'But, Leah....' The student was clearly at a loss.

'Tell me what's troubling you, Jennifer.'

'Jenny.'

'Sorry, Jenny. I forgot.'

'That's all right. I just think it all sounds daft. I mean, kings riding horses and that.'

Leah smiled. 'It's the sport of kings, Jenny. Anyway, it's supposed to be daft. The whole premise of the play is daft.'

'Well, how are we going to keep crowns on our heads when we're going through all the steps?'

'Oh, I expect we'll find some glue somewhere. Right, everyone, let's get started.'

Two hours later, at Easingthorpe Primary School, Sylvia was rehearsing her children's chorus.

'Take it from where Dick finds his ship deserted,' she said. 'Ready? "How can I go anywhere when I have no crew?" ' She waited five seconds and said, 'You missed your cue, children. You have to run on stage immediately and say, "We'll be your crew, Dick." Let's try again. Ready? "How can I go anywhere when I have no crew?" '

The children took their cue and ran towards her, shouting, ' "We'll be your crew, Dick!" '

' "But surely you're not real sailors." '

' "We'll show you!" '

Freddy played the introduction to 'The Sailors' Hornpipe', and the children gathered in a line.

'No,' said Sylvia. 'Dress with intervals, as I showed you. Stick your right arm out sideways until the tips of your fingers touch your neighbour's shoulder, and then shuffle your feet until you're just the right distance apart.'

The little boy at the end of the line said, 'Mrs Hinchcliffe, I haven't got anybody to touch.'

'Of course you haven't. Just stand to attention and show everyone how smart you are.'

Eventually, the hornpipe began, with Sylvia prompting the children with each sequence, until they came to the rocking step.

'Stop everybody. I've shown you all how to do this. Let's practice the step. One, two, three, four.' It wasn't happening as it should, so she removed her shoes and put them on a gymnastics bench by the wall. 'Now, watch while I do it slowly for you.'

After several tries, they got the idea and performed the horn-pipe from the beginning, and to Sylvia's cautious satisfaction.

'Now, children, as you pass Dick to go on board his ship, you have to salute him.'

Inevitably, some of the boys tried clowning it, but none of them had any idea.

'No, like this. Watch me. The palm faces downward. No, that's silly. You're exaggerating it.' She tried again. 'The palm downward and the wrist slightly bent.' She closed her eyes at their efforts and counted up to ten. 'Mr Hinchcliffe will show you. His hands are bigger than mine.'

Freddy left the piano, possibly wondering what the size of his hands had to do with the quality of his demonstration. 'Right, kids,' he said, 'get this right, because it's important. Short way up, palm down, wrist bent slightly. Hold it there.' He walked down the line, correcting each child's salute. 'Okay, short way down. Let's try it again. Short way up, short way down. Well done.'

They practised marching past Sylvia and saluting, until she was quite pleased with the result.

As their parents took them home, she said, 'I can't be stern with them like you, Freddy. They're only children.'

'Nonsense. Scare the wits out of them, That's the only way to do it.' He was smiling and, in any case, she knew he didn't mean it.

On Tuesday morning, Gavin had a new second-study piano student, a girl called Deborah Giles, who had apparently made herself unpopular with the visiting lecturer originally allocated to her. Jonathan had been characteristically vague about the reason for their disagreement.

She arrived for her lesson, wearing a Mexican peasant blouse, frayed jeans and, incredibly, wooden clogs. Her hair was unkempt and possibly dirty.

'Good morning, Deborah,' he said. 'What are you going to play for me?'

'*Serenade for the Doll.*'

'From Debussy's *Children's Corner,*' he prompted. 'It's sometimes useful to have the full title.'

She merely nodded.

'Be my guest.' He indicated the piano.

She placed her music on the desk and took her place at the piano. After peering at the music, as if it were a total surprise, she began.

Her playing was questionable, but not beyond help, and he was about to make certain suggestions, when the general effect was marred completely by a sustained left hand note that bore no relation to the harmonies that followed. A glance at her feet confirmed his suspicion.

'Deborah, stop for a moment, please.'

'There's something wrong with this piano,' she told him confidently.

'Have you never played a Steinway before?'

'No, and if they're all like this, I won't be in a hurry to play one again.' Her tone was reminiscent of an angry housewife in a badly-run store.

'If you haven't, you won't be familiar with the third pedal,' he pointed out.

She looked down, evidently noticing it for the first time. 'Do you mean the one in the middle?'

'Yes, the *sostenuto* pedal. It sustains one note in the bass without affecting any of the others. It's quite useful for some pieces. Unfortunately, you pressed it instead of the damper pedal, hence the bum note that wouldn't go away.'

'Well, now I know it's there, can I carry on?'

'Please do.' He would save his suggestions for later.

She began the piece again, but it wasn't long before the *sostenuto* pedal re-entered the proceedings.

'It's done it again,' she said, as if the piano had done it by malicious design.

'Yes, I can't help thinking that if you're going to wear clogs it might be a good idea to bring shoes to change into. I'm thinking of something more practical.'

'These cost me thirty quid.'

'I've no doubt they're of the highest quality, Deborah, but they're not ideal in this case. In certain applications, they're probably indispensable, but let's be realistic. You've come here to play the piano, not to milk a cow.'

'That does it.' She snatched her music and made for the door. 'You're as bad as that other feller.'

———

As he was about to go to lunch, Jonathan hailed him from his office.

'Gavin, a word, if you would.'

'This wouldn't be about Deborah Giles, would it?'

'Yes, it would. You know, Gavin, you really must treat your students more sensitively. The poor girl was positively enraged.'

Gavin nodded. It was as he'd expected. 'Are you at all interested in hearing my side of the story, Jonathan?'

'Of course I am.'

'Good, because whatever she told you, all I did was to suggest she brought some more practical footwear to her lesson.'

'She was beside herself, Gavin. You must be more accommodating. These people are very young.'

'Is that all, Jonathan?'

'Yes, as long as you remember what I've said.'

'I always do. Good day to you.' Lunch beckoned. It was an opportunity to escape from the Music School for an hour.

By the time he'd reached Robshaw's Tea Room, any thoughts he might have had about healthy eating had evaporated, and he ordered sausages and baked beans on toast with a poached egg on top.

He escaped censure because, on that occasion, Leah failed to materialise. He concluded that she must be engaged in something important.

On Wednesday morning, he found Jonathan in a state of near apoplexy.

'I had an organ lesson with that girl,' he fumed.

'Which girl was that, Jonathan?'

'Deborah Giles, the student who complained about you.'

'Oh, yes? A lovely girl, too.'

Jonathan was shaking. 'She came for an organ lesson,' he said, 'wearing *clogs*!'

'She's very proud of them, Jonathan. They cost her a lot of money.'

'I don't care if they cost her the National Debt. I told her straight, she can't play the organ in clogs.'

Gavin looked suitably sympathetic. He said, 'I imagine you, she and J S Bach went on to spend a rewarding hour together?'

'No, we didn't. She walked out on me.'

'Oh, Jonathan.' Gavin shook his head sadly. 'You really must be more... what's the word I'm looking for? I had it a moment ago. Yes, *accommodating*. We have to be sensitive to the needs of our students. After all, they're very young.'

Jonathan's response was unusually profane for an organist, but Gavin didn't care. He had other considerations, chief among which was a Country and Western song to be sung by King Edward the Seventh.

16

KING EDWARD THE SEVENTH:

INTRO: I was a prince for sixty years, the envy of my peers,
'Though the benefit was hard to recognise.
It was a long old time to wait, for a future head of state,
And temptation came a-callin' in this wise.

VERSE: My nanny used to say, 'Hey, put that thing away,
It'll cause a heap o' trouble one fine day,'
But I said, 'I mean to use it. If I don't, I'll likely lose it,
An' heirs don't get made any other way.'

CHORUS: I chose a life with the ladies, and the rest could go to Hades.
Even royal princes have a need.
An' I didn't do it lightly, but I aimed for three times nightly,
And to make it less than that was rare indeed!

I lived a life filled with jollity, with mistresses of quality,
An actress and a hostess 'mong the rest.
Miss Langtry, known as Lily, was the toast of Piccadilly,
And Mrs Keppel ranked among the best.

CHORUS: I chose a life etc.

Soon, my deeds were in the news, and Gladstone aired his views,
'Bout the ladies I've referred to in this song,
And my escapades and capers, 'til my ma succumbed to vapours,
And ordered me to end my tale of wrong.

CHORUS: I chose a life etc.

When I came to the throne, I tried hard to atone,
For my weaknesses for wine and food and wenches,
But, as statesman, I soon found my repute had gotten 'round,
And my stock was ridin' high with the Frenchies!

CHORUS: I chose a life etc

INSTRUMENTAL [24 bars]

But since my sad demise, I'm obliged to sever ties,
With the ladies of my past and wanton life,
And adopt a pure existence, with the precept and assistance,
Of my dear, forgiving, understanding wife!

CHORUS: I chose a life etc.

Gavin placed the manuscript in a folder, ready to give to Clare in the morning for typing. Meanwhile, he and Leah had a meeting with Neil.

They went through the rehearsal schedule for the coming week without contention but, when Gavin showed Neil the manuscript of the Edward the Seventh song, he seemed unconvinced.

'It has an American feel to it,' he said.

'So it should. It's a Country and Western song.'

'Is that a good idea, Gavin?'

'I hope so. It works for me.'

Neil was still undecided. 'Aren't you being a little ambitious?'

'I hope we all are. That's if we intend to make any progress in this life.' He saw Leah roll her eyes, and was tempted to do the same.

'Gavin love—'

'Just "Gavin", remember?'

'Sorry, it's a difficult habit to break. Isn't Country and Western somewhat exotic?'

'Last time I looked at a map, it was, yes. If I remember rightly, it comes from the other side of the Atlantic.'

Neil bridled almost theatrically. 'There's no need to be sarcastic, love.'

'Who?'

'Sorry. All I'm trying to say is that our resources are limited to what we have here, and it seems to me that Country and Western is a sophisticated and demanding kind of music.'

'So is classical music, but we have every confidence that the penny will eventually drop with our students.'

'Gavin, let me put it simply. Where are you going to find the musicians to accompany the song?'

Gavin's patience was almost exhausted. 'To answer your question simply,' he said, 'in the Music School, where there are several classical guitar students capable of doubling on the banjo and, if necessary, even the dulcimer.'

'I was only asking for clarification.'

'In your inimitable way,' added Leah, who had been quiet until then. 'If you're satisfied that Gavin knows what he's doing, and you should be by this time, I have a point to raise.'

'Suddenly, sarcasm is all the rage. What is your point, Leah love?'

'Just "Leah", thank you.'

'Oh, the bitterness of life.' He sighed deeply. 'What is it, Leah?'

'On looking through my copy of the script, I find that the final scene is missing. Can you let me have a copy?'

'No, dearest, I can't, simply because it doesn't yet exist.'

Leah looked astounded. 'Why ever not?'

'Because I haven't written it yet.'

It was Leah's turn to gather her patience. 'Neil,' she said, 'Gavin and I need to work on it, the students need to rehearse it and, presumably, you need to set it on stage. Don't you feel that it might be a good idea, as a matter of urgency, to put pen to paper? We don't even know, at this stage, who's going to win the election to the Upper Chamber.'

For the first time, Neil looked uncomfortable. 'That's the problem,' he confessed. 'I haven't decided yet.'

For a moment, Leah and Gavin were speechless. Then Gavin said, 'You could always toss a coin.'

'Gavin dear—'

'Just "Gavin", as I have to remind you yet again.'

'Leave it with me. I'll write the bloody scene.'

'Good,' said Leah, standing up to leave, 'but do get on with it. The suspense is killing.'

Gavin picked up the manuscript of the song and left with her. When they were outside, he asked, 'D' you fancy a drink?'

'I think we both need one. The Duke's Head?'

'Where else?'

They walked the short distance to the pub.

Gavin asked, 'What's your poison?'

'Neil is, but I'd like a glass of dry white, and it's my turn to buy them.'

He found a table while Leah bought the drinks.

She placed her wine and a pint of bitter on the table. 'Aren't you eating here tonight?'

'Not unless you fancy it.'

She shook her head. 'I have a cottage pie that needs to be eaten. How about you?'

'I've got something prepared,' he said.

'D' you mean you've found your can opener?'

He nodded self-consciously. 'It was hiding at the back of the drawer,' he said. 'It was most embarrassing.'

'Let's change the subject. I've got you a ticket for the pantomime.'

'Thank you. I'm looking forward to that.' He reached for his wallet and asked, 'What do I owe you?'

'Nothing. I said I'd *got* you a ticket. I didn't say I'd paid for it.'

'Which night?'

'Saturday. They're only doing it on Friday and Saturday nights, with a matinee on Saturday afternoon. More than that would be too much for the children, not to mention my mum and dad.'

Gavin blinked at the thought. 'I don't know how they do it,' he said.

'This could be the last. They're beginning to feel the strain, and they're no longer young.'

'They don't look all that old.'

Leah thought briefly. 'My mum's fifty-one and my dad's fifty-six.'

They both fell silent, wondering how it must feel to be as old as that.

'There'll be a party of us,' said Leah eventually. 'Bailey, Elaine and Janice are coming. They'll sit on the end of the row so that Janice can get to the loo. She tends to laugh uncontrollably at pantomimes, and there's only one consequence.'

'I know,' he said. 'I'm the same.'

'In that case, you're not going to sit next to me.'

'All right. I'll sit with Janice. We'll have something in common.'

With that settled, Leah asked, 'Are you doing much at Christmas?'

'I don't imagine so. Once Santa's been, there's not a lot to do, really.'

'We usually sit in front of the telly and cringe every time my dad says, "I wonder when they're going to show *Holiday Inn* again." '

'I'm with him there,' said Gavin, instantly aroused. 'They haven't shown it for years.'

'I prefer *Blue Skies*, if we're talking about Fred and Bing.'

'Otherwise, which is your favourite Fred film?'

'This is a game men play, isn't it?' Nevertheless, she gave the question some thought and said, '*Carefree*. Your turn.'

'*Top Hat*.'

'I thought it might be. It shows Ginger Rogers at her fluffiest and most appealing to men.'

Suddenly, Gavin remembered something. 'I'll tell you something about Ginger Rogers,' he said.

'Go on, spill the beans.'

'When Frank Morrison and I were students, he went one day to the Coliseum to get some tickets. Anyway, he took the wrong route and found himself in Drury Lane, outside the Theatre Royal.'

'The wrong theatre, poor chap.'

'Yes, and the big production there was *Mame*, starring Ginger Rogers. Well, Frank was standing there, looking at the poster, when the stage door opened, and Ginger Rogers stepped outside.'

'No.'

'Frank was desperate to meet her, but he was so shy in those days, especially with women, that his feet wouldn't budge.'

'That's tragic.'

'Yes, and then a minicab arrived, and she got in. It was all over for Frank. He was in a daze for the rest of the week.'

Leah looked at her watch and said, 'That was a very sad story, Gavin, but it's time for me to go. Don't feel that you have to leave as well.'

'But I must. The can opener beckons.' He held the door for her to leave.

'Are you going to offer me your arm again?'

'Of course I am. It's available all the year round, you know.'

She took his arm. 'You're disconcertingly nice, Gavin.'

'What's disconcerting about me?'

'Just the fact that you're so nice.'

'And you haven't known many nice men. I remember now.'

They walked as far as her car.

'Thanks for the drink and the pantomime ticket.'

She laughed. 'You're welcome.'

He leant forward to kiss her cheek just as she turned her head, and their lips brushed accidentally.

'I'm sorry,' he said.

'Don't be.' She inclined her head for him to kiss her cheek.

'See you tomorrow.'

'Be careful with that can opener.' She got into her car and started the engine. He waited until she was safely away.

17

Christmas at the Hinchcliffe household was the cheerful event it had always been, but with one special ingredient. *Holiday Inn*, starring Bing Crosby and Fred Astaire, was shown on Christmas Eve, a programming decision that Leah's father regarded as a personal gift and one to be treasured. Leah would have preferred *Blue Skies*, but she was pleased for her excited parent, unlike Martin, who couldn't see the point in either film. Leah reminded him that it had made their dad happy, and that no other justification was necessary.

On Boxing Day, Leah, Martin and Wendy Albright went to the Shearer's Arms where, loquacious as ever, Wendy failed to notice Martin's reluctance to add to the conversation, until he left the lounge bar to answer a call of nature, and Leah was free to raise the subject.

'He's terribly shy,' she said. 'That's why conversation is such hard work.'

'Is he?' Wendy gave the phenomenon a moment's consideration and asked, 'What has he got to be shy about, a clever lad like him? He was always clever at school, I remember. I thought he was quiet because he spent a lot of time thinking, the way clever people seem to.'

'He probably doesn't realise how able he is,' said Leah, fearing that the word 'clever' might soon be claiming overtime. 'Some people don't.'

Wendy nodded slowly, as if Leah's suggestion might explain a great deal. 'I used to think he fancied me a bit,' she said, sweeping a lock of dark hair from her eyes. 'I used to catch him looking at me sometimes.'

'He probably still does, Wendy. He's just too shy to make contact with you.' She leaned forward to say confidentially, 'He's looking forward to seeing you in the pantomime.' He hadn't mentioned it, but it was a fair bet, considering the view that would be on offer.

'Is he? Maybe I should wear fishnets more often. Some of the lads at work say I should. Mind you, they have just one thing on their minds, the dirty buggers.'

'It might help. You never know.' In the perverse way of things, Wendy was wearing a voluminous maxi dress that her parents had bought her for Christmas, and her prime assets were hidden from view. 'There's something else that might help, although probably not on the same day.'

'What's that?'

'You could find a shared interest.'

'Yeah? What is he interested in?'

'Ornithology.' To avoid misunderstanding, she added, 'Birdwatching. According to my dad, Martin's quite passionate about it.'

Her suggestion had given Wendy cause for thought. That was evident, because she was quiet, and that only happened when she was thinking.

'It'll have to wait 'til after the pantomime,' said Wendy thoughtfully, 'but I'll give it a try.' On further reflection, she said, 'I am interested in nature, and I'll try most things if it'll help me find out if there really is life on Mars, and not just in the song.'

'Shh, he's coming back.'

Martin eyed the empty glasses on the table and asked, 'Same again?'

'Yes, please.'

'Yeah, please, Martin.'

'He spoke two words,' observed Leah as he went to the bar. 'That's going some for him.'

'I think he just needs encouraging,' said Wendy, sounding like someone ever-confident of a result.

'There's something else I've been meaning to ask you.'

'What's that, Leah?'

'Are you going to do that thing when Dick Whittington loses his cat and goes into the auditorium, looking for him?'

Wendy laughed. 'Yes, but I'm not going to ask if anyone's seen my pussy. Judith Richardson did that a few years ago, and it brought the house down.'

'It would.' Coming from someone with Judith's reputation, it was also a silly question. 'No, I was wondering if you were going to do the usual thing, and take him to meet some of the children in the audience.'

'Yes, a stroke and a cuddle always go down well.' She smiled at Martin as he put the drinks on the table. 'Don't you think so, Martin?'

'What?'

'Children always like to stroke a pantomime cat.'

'Oh.'

'The thing is,' said Leah, 'you've met Bailey, haven't you?'

'Bailey?' Wendy narrowed her eyes in thought, and then realisation came. 'Oh yes, he stepped in as Captain Hook when Jack Thornton caught the shingles. He was great.'

'Yes, that's Bailey. Once experienced, never forgotten.'

'What about him?'

'He'll be there with his wife and daughter. Now, his daughter Janice is a nice girl. She's about our age, but she has Down's syndrome. You know....'

'I know, I met her when Bailey was Captain Hook.'

'Oh, good.' It made things easier. 'I don't know how the girl who's playing Tom would feel about this, but Janice would be terribly disappointed if she didn't get a visit. She was distraught after the Three Bears left her out.'

Wendy nodded with the wisdom of an experienced pantomime actress. 'Don't worry, Leah. Let me know where they'll be sitting, and I'll bring Tom to her. Amanda's okay with that kind of thing. Her mum works at the special school.'

Leah was happy. It had been a useful evening.

Back at the college, Gavin had completed three more chorus numbers, a rock ballad for King Gustavus Adolphus of Sweden, and a gentle lullaby for Tsar Peter the Great of Russia.

'I can see you've been busy,' observed Leah. 'Did you find time to have a good Christmas?'

'Very good, thank you. Did your dad see *Holiday Inn*? I did.'

'He did, and I've no doubt we'll hear about it on a yearly basis, until they show it again.'

'He may not have long to wait. According to one of the technicians working on the theatre lights, video recorders and players in private homes may soon become a reality, and I'm sure the film studios will be only too ready to swamp the market with classic films.'

Leah smiled as a thought occurred to her. 'That'll present my dad with a fascinating dilemma. He's a confirmed luddite where technology's concerned. He used to go bonkers every time Harold Wilson mentioned the "white heat of technology".'

'I felt the same.' Gavin dismissed the memory and asked, 'Apart from *Holiday Inn*, then, how was your Christmas?'

'Very nice, really and, as a bonus, I've set the wheels in motion to fix up my brother with the girl who lives across the road from my parents.'

'The girl who doesn't close her curtains?'

She gave a tired sigh, and said, 'I've told you about her, obviously.'

'Yes, but she remains a tantalising mystery. I mean, how would you describe her?'

Leah had to think. 'Without being bitchy,' she said eventually, 'I'd say she's an uncomfortable reminder of how ballet robs a woman of her man-appeal.'

'How does it do that?'

'It gives us calloused feet, muscles and a flat chest. On the other hand, Wendy has soft curves in all the right places, the kind of legs that got her the principal boy part in the pantomime, and a respectable bust measurement. Oh, and she's quite pretty as well.'

Gavin looked thoughtful. He asked, 'What else?'

'You want more? Okay, she's very friendly, but she only ever stops talking to eat, think or, I can only imagine, to brush her teeth.'

'In that case, your brother's welcome to her.'

'She has nice teeth.'

'I don't care. I can't cope with a chatterbox.'

'Maybe there's hope for the rest of us.' It was a cheering thought, and one that she took with her to her next class.

Gavin had a piano lesson with Clive, the pleasant student who was studying Beethoven's First Piano Sonata. He seemed to have something on his mind.

'Gavin,' he said, 'Mr Bright says Liszt's music is vulgar and vacuous.'

'When did he say that?'

'A few weeks ago, and he mentioned it again this morning in harmony.'

It struck Gavin as ironic that Paul Bright, one of the older lecturers, who disapproved of first names between staff and students, should teach harmony, when he was one of the least harmonious characters in the place.

'I wonder what prompted that.'

'Only that I said I had to get away for a piano lesson.'

'Ah.' Gavin was no stranger to the petty rivalries and jealousies that were a feature of music school life, and he knew that Bright's observation was prompted by his lunch-hour recital programme. 'Well,' he said, 'it's true that much of his music is very technical – Liszt was probably the greatest piano virtuoso of all – and he didn't function as most composers did. For one thing, he didn't develop his themes in the way that Beethoven did, and that puts him beyond the pale as far as most pundits are concerned.'

'Why do you play his music, then?'

'Because I like it, at least, most of it. If a piece is rewarding to play and entertaining to listen to, it doesn't matter to me that it's not written in the best traditions of Bach, Mozart or Beethoven.'

'I see.'

'Good, so let's hear the Beethoven.'

Clive had reached the bottom of the second page, when Gavin stopped him. 'It's sounding good,' he said, 'but you're making it hard work for yourself, and you're not producing the fullest tone. Let's swap places for a minute.'

He took his place at the piano and said, 'You're playing it like this.' He demonstrated, using Clive's flat hand technique. 'Compare that with this.' He played the same section, using his wrists to get the required weight over each note. Finally, he asked, 'What difference did you notice?'

'Yours sounded better.'

'Good. Anything else?'

'You didn't play with a flat hand.'

'I should think not. There was a time when some of the old ducks teaching piano used to lay coins on their pupils' hands, telling them they must keep their hands perfectly flat and not let the coins slide off.'

'I was taught like that.' It was almost a confession.

'It wasn't your fault, but I'm surprised you've gone so long without injury. The flat hand thing is a recipe for tenosynovitis.'

'What's that?'

'A horrible lurgy you're much better without. Now, have you seen the advertisement for Yellow Pages, the one that says, "Let your fingers do the walking"?'

'Yes.'

'Well, try to forget it. Instead, think of letting your wrists carry your fingers to where they need to be. The wrist is the most versatile joint in the human body and much stronger than the fingers, so let's start using it to our best advantage.'

Teaching could be very rewarding, and it wasn't the only pleasure Gavin would enjoy that week, because on Saturday, he would relive a childhood treat at the pantomime.

18

asingthorpe Town Hall was full, which said much for the
popularity of Yoredale Players. Friday had been a good house
and the Saturday matinee had attracted schools from a wide
area, but Saturday night drew the biggest house of all.

Bailey was his usual urbane self, introducing Gavin to Elaine
and Janice, and then to Martin, who had little to say, but Leah had
prepared him for that. Peering over the band screen, Gavin iden-
tified several of the 'Dalesmen'. Freddy and Sylvia were naturally
backstage, but he would see them later, after the performance.

The house lights were dimmed, and Freddy walked to the rostrum to generous applause. He was evidently a popular figure in
Easingthorpe.

Then began a *pot-pourri* overture of various popular numbers
from the past twenty years or so. Eventually, the curtain rose on
a number of citizens, aldermen, children and sundry townsfolk.
Inevitably, they were singing a song about a holiday and, hackneyed
though the convention was, Gavin was nevertheless reminded of
the pantomime thrill he'd known in childhood.

As the chorus dispersed, Dick Whittington made his entrance,
with his worldly goods contained in a red-spotted handkerchief
tied to a stick. However, those were not the assets that attracted
Gavin's attention.

Leah whispered, 'See what I mean?'

Gavin saw what she meant.

Dick sang 'Around the World'. She had an attractive voice, too.
Gavin gave Leah's hand an encouraging squeeze, just in case it were
needed.

Dick's initial lines to the audience were interrupted by a bang on the bass drum, a red spotlight, and a horrible figure that leapt out of the wings.

'Daddy!' The cry came from Janice at the end of the row.

'It's all right, darling,' said Bailey, who knew a thing or two about pantomime villains. 'Fairy Bow-Bells and Dick will put the blighter in his place. Just you see.'

'Allow me to introduce myself, Whittington,' said the verminous intruder. 'I am King Rat and it is my purpose to foil your plans.'

Gavin took Leah's hand again.

'I'm not scared,' she said.

'I am.'

A white spotlight came on to pick out a pretty girl in a white, classical tutu and bodice.

'Begone, King Rat,' she commanded, assisted ably by an audience of hissing children, 'for I, Fairy Bow-Bells, am here to protect Dick Whittington in his quest for fame and fortune.'

'I'll be back,' promised the rodent. 'Fairy Bow-Bells won't always be around, Whittington.' Then with a horrible laugh, he leapt into the wings.

It seemed that Fairy Bow-Bells meant business, because her next good deed was to find a friend and companion for Dick. His new help-mate was to be none other than Tom, a big black cat, who capered around the stage to everyone's delight before taking his place at Dick's heel.

Gavin peered at Martin, who was staring, open-mouthed, at Dick. It was just possible that Leah might yet be successful in her sisterly scheme.

Sarah the Cook and Idle Jack the Scullery Boy performed the obligatory slapstick kitchen sketch, which ended with flour all over the floor and Elaine taking Janice to the ladies' room, such was the effect of her laughter at the clowning on stage. Martin appeared to have lost interest in the pantomime, if only for the time being.

When King Rat appeared in his usual red spotlight to steal the Alderman's gold, Janice jumped at the bang on the bass drum but, with apparent trust in Bailey's judgement, she soon settled down.

Now, banished from the Fitzwarren home and London itself,

Dick arrived at the docks to find a ship that could carry him abroad. He found one, but it was deserted.

He asked the audience, 'How can I go anywhere when I have no crew?' It was a fair question, but then a party of children in sailor suits ran on to the stage and volunteered *en masse* for service at sea. They established their credentials by dancing an impressive hornpipe before boarding the ship.

At the start of the second act, Tom went missing. Dick was distraught, searching the ship without result, and then turning in desperation to the audience.

'Has anyone seen Tom, my cat?'

Leah was shaking with silent laughter. Eventually, she said to Gavin, 'I'll tell you later.'

Tom appeared upstage and in a playful mood.

The children shouted, 'He's behind you!' The rest was pantomime protocol, but Dick eventually found him and brought him into the auditorium to meet the children. Good as her word, Wendy took him to Janice to administer the essential hug while Martin stared in fascination.

Then came the shipwreck, followed by the scene in the Sultan's Palace with a clever, eastern-style dance routine, and the defeat of the rats, which had swarmed all over Marrakesh. And so, Dick and Tom returned to Blighty, liberally rewarded for their efforts but, even so, they were not yet welcome in the nation's capital.

Sadly, Dick walked away from London until it was time to sit down and rest.

'Oh, Tom,' said Dick, 'now I can never go back to London and marry Alice.' They both nodded off, and that was the cue for Fairy Bow-Bells to wake them up. It occurred to Gavin that, in similar circumstances, he might have resented having his forty winks cut to ten or less, but Dick Whittington did have a vested interest in hearing what Fairy Bow-Bells had to say.

'Listen, Dick,' she said. 'Listen to the bells of Bow.'

As Dick listened, the bells acquired human, backstage voices. They were singing, 'Turn again, Whittington, thou worthy citizen. Turn again, Whittington, Lord Mayor of London Town.'

So, it was back to London, and – Gavin guessed it – another

plague of rats. King Rat had escaped the Massacre of Marrakesh and raised another regiment of rodents in London.

It was an ugly scene, with the rats singing an ugly song. Dick and Tom, victors of Marrakesh, stood poised, padded up and ready for the home fixture.

Dick said, 'Get 'em, Tom!'

Once again, Tom dispatched a number of rats with a right hook here, a straight left there, and an occasional uppercut, possibly for variety, until King Rat stood alone, defiant.

Gavin took Leah's hand again.

'It'll be all right,' she told him. 'Trust me, I've seen it before.'

King Rat roared, 'You can't hurt me, Whittington!'

'Oh, can't I?' Dick drew his sword, King Rat drew his, and they circled each other. Meanwhile the children hissed and cheered alternately. The fight began under flashing strobe lights, and continued in such a convincing way that Martin was perched on the edge of his seat. Dick eventually triumphed, and King Rat lay on the ground, defeated.

'Told you,' said Leah.

Martin looked on, entranced.

Eventually, the curtain rose to reveal Dick in his mayoral chain, Alice, Tom, Alderman Fitzwarren and the rest of the cast. There was a musical finale, and Sylvia walked on stage to be given a bouquet and a well-deserved round of applause. Finally, Freddy took a bow and brought the musicians to their feet to do the same. It had been a highly successful production.

'Well,' said Gavin, 'I enjoyed that.'

'Except when you were scared,' said Leah.

'I wasn't really scared.'

'Oh, no?' Her tone suggested disbelief.

'Not at all. I just like holding your hand.'

'You quaint, old-fashioned thing.' She stood up to follow Martin, Bailey and the others, saying, 'We're all going to the end of show party at the Shearers' Arms. It's only next door.'

It sounded like a good idea, so he joined the line making its exit from the Town Hall.

The Shearers' Arms was already quite crowded, but Bailey, who was taller than anyone in the bar, had no difficulty in attracting the landlord's attention.

'You can't get all these, Bailey,' said Gavin.

'Of course I can, dear boy. Time spent with the Hinchcliffe dynasty, and particularly after such a triumph, is worth celebrating.' Looking towards the entrance he saw Freddy and Sylvia arriving. 'Ah, Freddy and Sylvia. The usual?' He placed his order, which included two pints of Theakston's Bitter for Freddy, because he knew from long experience how long the first would last.

'Well, ladies and gentlefolk,' said Bailey when the group was assembled, 'this has been another in a long line of Hinchcliffe successes. Well done, both.' He handed a gin and tonic to Sylvia and a pint of bitter to Freddy, who relieved the inner drought by downing it in one grateful swallow. Bailey casually handed him the next.

'Thanks, Bailey. You're sensitive as ever to a chap's needs.'

'It was the least I could do, old man.'

'Really well done,' said Gavin. 'I'm full of admiration for you both.'

'Thank you,' said Freddy. 'It's good to know it was a success, as it will very likely be our last.'

'Oh.' The expression of disappointment came from Janice, who had been quiet hitherto, engaged as she was in downing a large glass of orange juice.

'You can't expect Uncle Freddy and Auntie Sylvia to go on doing these things for ever,' said Elaine. 'It's a big job, putting on a pantomime.'

'It's not just that,' said Freddy. 'Times change, and kiddies want pop music. If I'm honest, I really don't want to provide that.'

'Well, let's enjoy this year's success,' suggested Bailey.

They were doing that when Sylvia's sister Audrey arrived with her husband David, their sons and daughter having brought their children to the afternoon matinee.

'Well done, you two,' said Audrey. 'Bruce and Pauline said the matinee was excellent, and tonight certainly lived up to their recommendation. I've yet to hear from Andrew.'

'Here's Wendy,' said Leah, giving Martin a nudge. 'Go and get her a drink, Martin. Cinzano and lemonade with ice.'

'I know.' He pushed his way to the bar readily, leaving Leah to comment on his behaviour.

'It's unusual for Martin to remember anyone's favourite drink,' she commented. We can only await further developments.' She broke off to welcome Wendy to the group, now devoid of stage make-up and still bearing traces of moisturising cream. 'Well done, Wendy,' she said. 'Martin's getting you a drink.'

'Oh, bless him. I'm fair parched.'

'This is Gavin. We work together.'

'Hello, Gavin.'

'Hello and well done. I thought you were excellent.'

'Thank you. I'm glad you enjoyed it.'

Martin returned from the bar bearing a Cinzano and lemonade, which he gave to Wendy. 'Hello, Wendy,' he said.

'Thanks, Martin.' She leaned forward and kissed him on the cheek. 'I need this drink.'

Martin was blushing. Possibly to cover his embarrassment, he said, 'You were very good. I liked the fight.'

'Thank you. I enjoyed that too.' She put an arm round him and said, 'You know, you're really nice when you're not being so shy, and there's something I've been meaning to ask you, 'cause you're keen on wildlife, aren't you?'

'Yes.' He looked wary.

'It's all right, I just want to ask you about barn owls. We have a pair nesting in an old outhouse, where we used to keep gardening tools before we had to lock them up.'

Suddenly, Martin was looking at her with new interest.

'I sometimes hear this hissing noise, and I'm sure it's them, but why do they do it?'

Martin was happy to enlighten her. 'Hissing is usually about food,' he said, 'but at this time of year it's more likely to be a warning to predators.'

'What predators are there?' She seemed puzzled.

'Occasionally a buzzard, but it's more likely to be a fox. Mind you, a fox would have to be very hungry to attack an owl.'

Leah was staring at her brother in astonishment.

'A fox,' he went on, 'will always take the easy option if there is one. They're cowardly creatures, really, and they don't usually take on something that can fight back.'

'I'll get the drinks in,' said Gavin, conscious that closing time would soon be upon them.

When he'd found out what everyone was drinking, he went to the bar and was surprised to find Leah at his side.

'I can't believe it,' she said. 'That's the most I've heard him say to anyone.'

'It must be the fishnets,' concluded Gavin.

'She's certainly got a lot going for her.' She wrinkled her nose in thought. 'I wonder,' she said, 'if she's genuinely interested in barn owls.'

'Maybe they'll go bird-watching together.'

'I hope so. She'll be good for him.'

Gavin paid for the drinks, and they carried them back.

When they had all taken their drinks, Freddy asked, 'Aren't you having one, Gavin?'

'No, I have to drive home.'

'You're more than welcome to sleep on our studio couch,' said Sylvia.

'Thank you, Sylvia, but you're going to be busy enough without having a house guest to stay. No, I'll be on my way, but not before I've told you again how much I enjoyed the pantomime.'

'That's very kind of you, Gavin. Remember, you're always welcome, so come and see us again, won't you?' She gave Leah a meaningful look, which Gavin pretended not to notice.

He took his leave of the group. Martin and Wendy were busily discussing the hunting habits of the barn owl, so he decided not to interrupt. He looked around for Leah and found her behind him and making for the door.

'I'll walk with you to your car,' she said.

'Are you sure? It's very cold out there.'

'I'm tougher than you think.'

They left the pub, and she asked, 'Where are you parked?'

'In the market square. Just there.' He pointed to his car.

She took his arm and walked with him. 'I'm glad you came,' she said, her words coming through a cloud of vapour.

'I wouldn't have missed it for anything. It's been a special evening.'

'Special?'

'Your family have a way of making anything special.'

She smiled. 'Even Martin tonight.'

'Yes, I think something's beginning to happen there.'

They stopped when they reached Gavin's car. Leah stood facing him with her back to the driver's door, so he leaned forward to brush her cheek politely, as usual. As he did so, she responded by touching his lips with hers. He applied gentle pressure and found her reacting the same way. They probed and teased until, as if by unspoken agreement, they joined each other in an unhurried kissing embrace.

Eventually, she broke away to say, 'I'll see you on Monday.'

19

'**D**oes Louis the Fourteenth need a song?'

Neil stroked his chin affectedly as he considered the question. Eventually, he said, 'I doubt it. All the talk is *about* him rather than *from* him.' He picked up his script to read aloud. ' "That French Louis they call 'The Sun King' because 'tis widely asserted 'mong his courtiers that the sun shineth from within his fundament." No, Gavin, I don't think a song is necessary.'

'Queen Victoria, then?'

'She's important enough for one.'

'Okay.' Gavin made a note about Queen Victoria. 'That brings us to Bloody Mary,' he said. 'She's so incensed at the idea of Lady Jane Grey making her pitch, I think she needs one.'

'I agree.' Neil consulted his copy of the agenda, and said, 'What's the problem with the five.... I thought Henry the Eighth had six wives.'

'If you remember, Neil, you decided that Katherine Parr had no axe to grind, unlike the rest. Henry is ruled out in the early stages of the election, on the basis that he was immoral, a despot and the accuser of more than one innocent person. I just wondered if we should have a concerted number for them.'

'A what?'

'An ensemble, in this case, a quintet.'

'Why?'

'Because his wrongs have to be stated.'

'Do they?' Neil looked mystified.

'Surely you know your own play, Neil.' Leah showed it to him.

'It's a cast of thousands, darling. I can't be expected to remember everyone and everything.' He read the page from beneath the place where Leah was pointing, and said, 'All right, let them have their quintet.'

'I need to consult Leah, but I think it needs movement as well.'

'I'll be guided by you,' said Leah, 'as I've yet to hear it.' Then, picking up her copy of the script, she turned to Neil to ask, 'Have you written the last scene yet?'

'Give me a chance, darling. It was only just before Christmas that you raised the subject.'

'We're waiting, Neil, and time is running out.'

After the meeting, Gavin walked across to Leah's office before returning to the Music School.

'I'll swing for Neil,' said Leah. 'If you can write a song in an evening, he should surely be able to write the final scene without taking a sabbatical to do it.'

'I'm writing in whatever time I can grab. I have to take part in another lunch-hour recital, and that's involving me in a lot of work.'

'Another one, so soon?'

'This is with Naomi Rosenbaum. She teaches cello here and she wants us to play Rachmaninov's Sonata for Cello and Piano. I played it once before, but I have to practise it up again. It's every bit as difficult as any of his piano concertos.'

'Poor old you.' She paused in thought before asking, 'Could you take out one evening this weekend?'

'I'll probably need to.'

'In that case, come over on Saturday evening and I'll feed you. At the very least, it'll save you having to cook for yourself.'

⁓⁓⁓

QUEEN MARY TUDOR:

My anger burns like unquenched fire when I behold this lady,
This puppet of Northumberland, a parvenu and jade, she!
Nine days she ruled, and not one more, this impudent pretender,
A head of state as counterfeit as the Prisoner of Zenda!

Full proud, she sat upon the throne and held the orb and sceptre,

With fawning Privy Councillors to welcome and accept her.
But then, the Council turned against the Protestant heretic,
And cast its favour then on me in manner most pathetic.

They made me Queen, those sycophants, and now with crown instated,
  I gave the word that Lady Jane must be decapitated.
  For me, that power was meat and drink, I meant to use it freely,
  And rid the state of Henry's church I longed to do most dearly.

So, priests and bishops, deacons too, I burned with growing passion,
  Blasphemers and heretics all, I dealt with in this fashion.
  Am I remembered well for this? They call me 'Bloody Mary'!
  They crowned me Queen, expecting what? A vacuous vagary?

But now, I must achieve, before I meet my final doom,
  My object, to forbid Jane Grey to reach that Upper Room.
  For full four hundred years I've longed that such a chance come nigh,
  Let Bloody Mary's final act Jane's place above deny! [reaches for Jane's proposal as Stewards of the Hereafter place her in a strait-jacket and lead her away].

Gavin admitted to himself that it was possibly wrong of him to suggest the stage direction at the end of the song, but it was equally wrong of Neil to withhold the final scene, so his conscience was clear. He would go home and practise the Rachmaninov.

On Tuesday, he tackled the easier number, the quintet for Henry's wives. Fun was always easier to express than anger, bitterness and hatred.

KATHERINE OF ARAGON:
How dare that man submit his name?
ANNE BOLEYN:

What qualities can Henry claim?
JANE SEYMOUR:
Must he again the truth disclaim?
ANNE OF CLEVES:
He mocks us all; 'tis but a jest.
KATHERINE HOWARD:
If jest it be, we must attest.
ALL:
We must attest to Henry's sin; if truth be all, he must not win.

VERSE *[sedately, as a Tudor part-song]: Our sov'reign Henry, we accuse of baseness foul and wrong,*
His wanton deeds we now condemn in terms both clear and strong.
Because, as loyal wives, we bore our grievances too long,
We now oppose his elevation with this earnest song.

CHORUS *[playfully]: Oh, what a very fickle man was he,*
That faithless Henry Tudor.
He showed neither trust nor clemency,
To a wife when once he'd wooed her,
But put her lightly in the dock,
With indictments ever lewder,
To be sent to the headsman's dreadful block,
That shameful Henry Tudor!

And travelled he across the sea his weddings to arrange,
More oft than not, a settlement was signed in fair exchange,
And then, at drop of velvet cap, his bride he would estrange,
The Royal Prerogative, it seemed, empowered 'chop and change.'

CHORUS: *Oh, what a very fickle man etc*

Our lord would gather mistresses, most often by the bunch-ly,
And dine them, 'ere he whisked them off, to bed them after lunch-ly.
Wives were there but to make an heir, and that, no more than monthly,

140

ANN OF CLEVES:
A monthly visit? Lucky wives. With me, not even once-ly!

CHORUS: Oh, what a very fickle man etc.

KATHERINE OF ARAGON:
As Spanish monarch's daughter, I came and wedded he,
Great things were yet expected of his little nut tree.
ALL:
King Henry's boon companion, that precious little tree,
Was soon to prove an empty boast when heirs were meant to be.
KATHERINE OF ARAGON:
And what was worse, that member proud, I know you will agree,
That Scottish parlance doth describe it well as 'only wee'!

CHORUS: Oh, what a very fickle man etc

That braggart of the bed-chamber would boast of worthy nooky,
How hour 'pon hour 'mid moan and groan, his wilful pleasure
took he.
Like giant's hand, his four-post bed with mighty efforts shook he,
Whilst light o' loves, mid-climax, gasped, 'No man hath better
tupped me!
KATHERINE HOWARD:
Good sisters, would he boast likewise, whilst eye to eyeball look
ye,
But, hour 'pon hour did last? Forsooth! Two minutes, were we
lucky!

CHORUS: Oh, what a very fickle man etc.

Gavin took a last look at the manuscript before putting it away. He had three hours left for practice before the neighbours complained. After that, he could look forward to dinner with Leah at the weekend.

20

L eah came to the door in a blue paisley maxi dress. She was wearing her hair down with evening make-up. Knowing as little as he did about perfume, Gavin couldn't identify the one she was wearing, but it was the kind of fragrance he found almost addictive, like the bouquet of an expensive cognac. He kissed her and presented her with a bottle of *Chateau Beaune-Villages*.

'How lovely. Thank you, Gavin.' She stood back to let him in.

'This is nice,' he said, looking around him. 'I caught a quick glimpse on the night of the ruby wedding, but no more than that.'

'I was lucky to find it,' she agreed. 'What can I get you to drink?'

'I don't know. What are you drinking?'

'Dry fino sherry.'

'I'll have the same, if I may.'

She poured a glass for him, and asked, 'How's the practice going?'

'Pretty well. I'm about ready for Tuesday.' He took the sherry from her. 'Thanks.'

'I thought the recital was on Thursday.'

'It is, but I have a run-through with Naomi on Tuesday, just to see if we can stay on the same page.'

'Come and sit down.' She sat on the sofa and patted the place beside her. 'How would you describe the music you're playing?'

He thought briefly. 'Like most of Rachmaninov's instrumental music, I'd call it ecstatic. That's without being too explicit,' he added.

'Now you've whetted my appetite, what would you call it if you were being explicit?'

'I'd probably say it was climactic.'

Her eyes opened wide. 'Now I *am* looking forward to Thursday,' she said.

'Stravinsky described Rachmaninov as "six-feet-four of Russian gloom", but he had feelings and, like many of his compatriots, he wore his heart on his sleeve.' To rescue the conversation, he asked, 'What are we eating tonight?'

'The starter's liver *pâté*, and the main course is chicken with pineapple. The pineapple's not compulsory, by the way.'

'I like it. I like most things,' he admitted.

'Like my dad. He puts it down to having been a 'kriegie', a prisoner-of-war. Bailey's the same.'

'I like your folks. They're lovely people.'

'Thank you. And guess what.' There was fun in her eyes.

'Go on.'

'Martin's home this weekend to do some owl-watching with Wendy.'

'I knew she'd lead him astray with that costume. His eyes were popping out like organ stops at the pantomime.'

'Wendy's not without her charms,' she agreed.

'She's all right if you like that kind of thing.'

She eyed him playfully and asked, 'Are you going to tell me you prefer flat-chested ballerinas?'

'Not all of them. Not all at once, anyway.'

'No, you've got to be realistic.' She stood up and said, 'If you're ready to eat, I'll put the toast on for the *pâté*.' She disappeared into the kitchen and returned with a china bowl of *pâté*, which she placed on the table.

'That smells good. Which animal donated its liver?'

'The chicken.' She smiled apologetically and said, 'There's a chicken theme to this meal that wasn't strictly intentional. I was concentrating more on the detail than the big picture.'

'I'm happy, Leah. The chicken is one of my favourite creatures.'

'That's a relief. Take a seat and I'll get the toast.'

This time, she returned with a plate of toast, a corkscrew and a bottle of Chablis, which she handed to him. 'Would you like to open it?'

'Of course.' He plied the corkscrew and drew the cork.

'Now,' she said, lighting the candle on the table, 'help yourself to *pâté*, toast and butter while I pour the wine.'

He took a modest helping of *pâté*, asking, 'Did you make this?'

'Of course.'

'I'm sorry. I didn't mean to—'

She smiled at his confusion. 'That's all right. Lots of people buy things ready-made nowadays. I just prefer to make things myself.'

'You're very accomplished.'

'Ah well, when I came home from hospital the first time, when I was sixteen – no, I was seventeen by then – my parents worked hard at keeping me occupied. My dad, as I told you, got me playing the piano for his rehearsals, and my mum taught me to cook and bake.'

'She taught you well. This *pâté* is superb.'

'Thank you. There's a hefty measure of cognac in there.'

'I can taste it.'

She was thoughtful for a moment. 'You know,' she said, 'this is the first time I've entertained in ages.'

'You haven't forgotten how.'

'You always say the right things, Gavin. I found it off-putting at first.'

'Really? Why was that?'

She shrugged, and said, 'Some men are glib. They say what they think women want to hear, but you're honest. I just didn't know that when we first met.'

'I suppose I can understand that. In a drama environment, with people like Neil around, it's difficult to tell the genuine from the artificial.'

'It's not just the luvvies.' She paused, and it seemed she might be about to tell him something quite personal. Eventually, she said, 'I have to know a man very well before I can trust him.'

'Of course.' His thoughts returned to the conversation he'd overheard at the ruby wedding.

'You're not surprised, then?'

'You told me you'd known a few wrong 'uns.'

'It's true. The last one was awful. He was full of easy charm at first.'

Gavin nodded, realising where her story was leading.

'Then, if things weren't as he wanted them, he became aggressive. I don't mean physically; that would have been bad enough, but he played horrible mind games.'

'Psychological bullying.'

'That's right, it was horrendous, and I decided I could take no more, so I showed him the door. Even then I couldn't get rid of him. He kept turning up, like a recurring nightmare, until my dad had to throw him out.' She smiled at the memory and said, 'I've never seen my dad so angry.'

'He had good cause to be angry.'

The oven timer buzzed.

'That's the chicken,' said Leah, 'but have some more *pâté*, by all means.'

'No, I mustn't. It's excellent, but let's not go mad.'

She beamed at him and said, 'My mum's told everyone about your beautiful manners. I'll be back in a minute.' She disappeared into the kitchen and emerged with two dinner plates, each bearing a breast of chicken and several slices of pineapple. She made another trip to bring the potatoes and vegetables.

'I seem to have made an impression on your mum,' he said.

'Oh, you have. Help yourself to veggies and spuds, by the way.'

'Thank you. What's the sauce? It smells good.'

She poured more wine and said, 'Pineapple and a few other things.' She added awkwardly, 'I'm glad you like pineapple.'

'It might otherwise have been a problem,' he agreed, 'but we'd have sorted something out, I'm sure.'

When he'd helped himself, she said, 'You mustn't feel threatened in any way, but I have to warn you that my mum is a compulsive matchmaker.'

'Really?'

'Yes, and I'm a serial disappointment.'

Her single status made that self-evident, but he forbore to comment on that. Instead, he said, 'It's maybe as well if your last chap was a sample.'

'Well, you know the score now. I just thought I'd tell you.'

'You know, you can't blame your mum. It's what they do. By the way, this is very good. I've never had it served with pineapple.'

'It's an American recipe. They're into anything Hawaiian just now.'

'Even grass skirts?'

'Not that I've heard.' She patted the front of her dress and said, 'In any case, I thought I'd keep it traditional.'

'Much safer.'

'That's what I thought. More veggies?' She pointed to the dish.

'No, thanks.'

They chatted easily through the meal, until Leah asked, 'Would you like to finish the wine?' She picked up the bottle.

'I'd better not, thank you.'

'Aren't you keen on it?'

'It's very nice, but I have to drive home.'

'That's a shame.' She put the bottle down again. 'Do you really have to drive? I can put you up. It's no trouble.'

'I'm tempted.'

'There's ice cream in the fridge.'

He hesitated, and then shook his head. 'No, you can't tempt me with ice cream,' he said. 'I've eaten a lot already.'

'In that case, have another drink. Something different?'

'No, I'll stay with the wine, if I may.'

She poured the last of the wine into his glass. 'There,' she said, 'now you have to stay.'

He gave her a stern look. 'I know what you're after. You want me to do the washing up.'

'That's right, but you can leave it until morning. Would you like coffee?'

'I don't think so, thank you.'

'You're right. It just adds to the washing up. Let's stack these things in the sink.'

'Okay.' He picked up what he could and followed her into the kitchen, where she leaned over the sink to stack the dishes tidily. As she did so, he put his hands on her waist. 'That was a brilliant meal,' he said, scenting her hair shampoo for the first time and enjoying its fresh aroma.

'Thank you.'

She turned so that her face was only inches away from his,

and they kissed. After a minute or so, she said, 'We could carry on getting friendly here, but we'd be more comfortable upstairs.'

'You know the way, and I'm easily led.'

'Follow me.' She led the way upstairs to her bedroom, and said, 'I'm just going to the bathroom. There's a chair there you can use.'

He sat on the bed to remove his shoes and socks. His shirt and trousers he draped obediently across the chair.

Leah returned after a minute, unhooking her dress. Then, as she pulled it over her head, Gavin realised that she was wearing nothing beneath it. He also noticed, when she turned towards him, that her pubic mound was completely unadorned. He recalled vaguely from somewhere that dancers commonly waxed or shaved, but the realisation was still unexpected.

He held out his arms and drew her close, enjoying the intimate contact for the first time.

They sank on to the bed, still in each other's arms. After a while, he reached for the pocket of his trousers, but she whispered in his ear, 'There's no need.'

They kissed again slowly, enjoying the luxuries of time and seclusion. She ran her fingers through his chest hair, creating furrows, and he wondered a little at the pleasure it gave her.

He began to kiss her repeatedly, journeying slowly downward to the modest swell of her bosom, where his lips encountered a delightfully erect nipple, and her breath quickened as he celebrated his discovery.

Still breathless, she reached downward, exploring and discovering. After a while, she felt his hand brush hers as it followed the shallow contour of her abdomen as far as the mount of Venus, and he revelled in the novelty of its smoothness before wonders of a more complex kind lured him further.

Overwhelmed by the sensations he was arousing, she shifted closer until their upper bodies were in contact. He moved over her, and she arched her back upward to receive him.

Despite the curtains' best efforts, weak winter sunlight was penetrating the room. Gavin rubbed his eyes, adjusting to his surroundings, and realised that Leah was missing. After a while, he heard movement downstairs and his curiosity was satisfied.

A visit to the bathroom was pressing, so he made his way to the landing and looked around for it. There were only two other rooms on the floor, and he made the right choice straight away.

Having flushed the loo, he looked around, as he washed his hands, at the myriad objects to be found in most women's bathrooms he'd known. It was truly remarkable that they could need all those things. He could see creams, moisturiser, cleansing wipes, bath salts, bubble bath, cotton wool, epilation wax, cotton buds and nail polish remover.

Thankful, then, that nature had spared him such complications, he dried his hands and returned to the bedroom, confident that Leah would return there.

After a few minutes, he heard her footfall on the stairs, and she appeared in a white, towelling bathrobe. She was carrying two mugs.

'Good morning,' she said. 'Which do you prefer at this hour? Tea or coffee?'

'Good morning. Tea, usually, but I'll take whatever comes.'

'I thought you might. I've made tea. You don't take sugar, do you?'

'No, you remembered well.'

She placed a mug of tea on each of the bedside tables, removed her bathrobe and re-joined him.

'Ballet is a wonderful discipline,' he said, 'but, of course, you know that already. I'm finding out about it for the first time.'

'Were you practising your *barre* exercises while I was downstairs?'

'No,' he said seriously, 'I was only thinking that you can do things with your legs that border on pornographic.'

'You've seen nothing yet. I was only getting back into practice.'

'In that case, I hope you'll invite me again.'

'Of course I will,' she confirmed, 'you passed your audition with flying colours.' She smiled confidingly and said, 'My mum likes to think I'm a virgin, although she must have drawn her own conclusions by this time.'

'It was different in her day, wasn't it?'

'I'll say it was. From what I can gather, they either put it about as if their lives depended on it, or else they lived like nuns. My mum tells me she was a virgin when she stood at the altar, although she said it once in my dad's hearing, and I overheard him mutter he'd had to wait longer than that.' She smiled mischievously. 'Just reading between the lines, I get the impression that her period started on their wedding day, and consummation had to be postponed.'

'Nature can be cruel.' He felt that one of them should show some sympathy.

'Can't it just? On top of that, I kept them waiting ages.'

'Your time-keeping's still better than Neil's,' he observed. 'Goodness knows how long he must have kept his parents in suspense.'

'And look at what they got when it arrived. Seriously, though, my folks were close to despair. But shall I tell you something cool? My mum told me this in one of her expansive moments, although, even then, she was a bit embarrassed. I mean, I know we don't like to think of the oldies doing the horizontal rhumba, but – and this is absolutely true – I was actually conceived on the summit of Lady Hill, near Hawes. Do you know it?'

'The hill with the tall pines on top?'

'That's right. My dad thought it might be an enchanted place, like the one in *The House at Pooh Corner*, so he took my mum up there for a picnic and had his wicked way with her. They actually did it *al fresco*.'

'Well, good for him; in fact, good for both of them.' On reflection, he added, 'And I hope it was too.'

'Yes,' she agreed, 'I don't see why we should have all the fun. She snuggled up closer, and asked, 'Have you finished your tea?'

'Yes, thank you.'

'You're not in a hurry to leave, are you?'

He considered the question and said, 'I do need to be at work tomorrow. Do you have something in mind?'

21

'The Thomas Arne Theatre in the Strand is booked for Sunday, the second of May. We'll have a technical rehearsal in the morning, the dress rehearsal in the afternoon, and the performance will be in the evening.' Vincent put his notes on the table and said, 'It gives us three months minus the Easter holiday.'

Neil asked, 'Have Dropforge Productions been informed?'

'Of course.'

It was Gavin's turn to ask a question. 'What other places are going to feature in the documentary?'

'There aren't all that many offering performance arts studies. There's the East Lancashire Academy, as you can imagine, a couple in the south of England and us.'

Gavin nodded. It was always on the cards that the East Lancashire Academy would take part. They'd been the big name in performance arts for some time.

'As far as I know,' said Vincent, 'ours is the only production to be featured. The others will basically show what's on offer and possibly a week in the life of a PA student.'

'That's encouraging,' said Gavin.

Vincent looked down at his notes. 'So,' he said, 'what still remains to be done?' He looked first at Gavin.

'Two choruses, a concerted number, a solo number and the final scene. I should finish most of them in the next two weeks.'

'Excellent. Leah?'

'Everything's in progress, Vincent. I'll liaise with Gavin as he finishes the remaining numbers, and that only leaves the final scene.'

'The final scene seems to have become a serial topic. What's the story with that, Neil?'

Neil flipped unnecessarily through his copy of the script, and said, 'Suddenly I feel there's a target pinned to my back.'

'I'm only asking you for clarification,' explained Vincent.

'Well, the big excitement is that the final scene is yet to be written.' He spread his hands in a way that suggested that his colleagues were making much ado about a matter of little consequence.

'I see.' Vincent regarded him coldly. 'I suggest,' he said, 'that you attend to it as a matter of urgency. Your colleagues, not to mention a cast of inexperienced students, are waiting to work on it.'

'All right,' said Neil, tossing his head. 'I'll just have to make a decision about the eventual winner of the election.'

'Do you mean you haven't decided yet?' Vincent sounded incredulous.

'I'm a victim of the complexity I've created,' he complained. 'It's a cast of bloody thousands, Vincent.'

'So you're spoiled for choice.' Vincent ran his hands over his hair. 'Perhaps you should adopt a process of elimination. Bin the baddies and prioritise the goodies. Of course, I shouldn't need to tell you that. You're capable of working it out for yourself, but whatever process you choose needs to begin today.' He gave the last word special emphasis.

The Music School common room wasn't one of Gavin's favourite haunts, but he made a point of going in periodically, more to check his pigeonhole and the notice board for anything that affected him than for any social purpose.

He was reading the notice board when Paul Bright spoke to him.

'Are you ready for your lunch-hour, Lowe?'

'I suppose so, although it's come at a very busy time for me.' He remembered Bright's reported remarks to Clive about Liszt's music being vacuous, and a mischievous thought occurred to him. 'Actually, I have a rehearsal with Naomi this afternoon. You wouldn't care to stand in for me, would you? In fact, you could do the lunch-hour itself. That's as long as you don't find the music vulgar and vacuous.'

'Don't be ridiculous, Lowe. You know the Rachmaninov is fiendishly difficult. I imagine you've been practising it for at least a couple of months.'

'Two weeks, actually. As I told you, I'm very busy.'

Having won the point, Gavin left his astounded and confounded colleague to gather his meagre wits. His next class, in five minutes' time, was in composition, and that, after all, was his chief purpose at Nidderdale.

He made his way to his teaching room and waited until the class was assembled.

'Good morning,' he said. 'It's generally believed that Mozart disliked the flute, and if that were true, wouldn't it seem rather odd that he wrote some truly beautiful music for it and incorporated it to great effect in his orchestral compositions? The idea came originally from a letter to his father, in which he said he'd been commissioned to write a number of flute pieces. He followed this with "a thing I cannot stand." Now, I think he was actually saying that he couldn't bear the idea of writing repeatedly for one instrument, and not that he couldn't stand the flute itself. In translating documents from a bygone era, it's all too easy to mistake the writer's meaning.' He looked around the room at the intrigued expressions on his students' faces, and knew it was time to explain.

'We all have our favourite instruments,' he said. 'Some we like more than others, and some we find less than endearing. Let's go round the class and hear what your least, or maybe I should say *less*, favourite instruments are.' His eye fell on a student on the front row.

'The bagpipes,' said the student, looking around, presumably for reinforcement, should it become necessary.

'You know,' said Gavin, 'if this conversation were to take place in Scotland or Ireland, yours would be a most unpopular point of view.' He smiled at the burst of laughter from the others, and said, 'Actually, in legal terms, the bagpipes don't constitute a musical instrument, but a weapon of war, like the bugle, the cavalry trumpet or the military drum. However, that's enough said about the bagpipes, which are still dear to the hearts of many, and we have to respect that. Let's hear from someone else.'

Another student said, 'The saxophone.'

'Do you mean all of them? Don't forget there's a whole family of saxophones.'

'No.' The girl seemed flustered. 'Just the one they use in jazz.'

'I think you mean the E flat alto sax, although others are used in jazz. Oddly enough, it's one of my instruments.'

'I'm sorry.' The girl looked very uncomfortable.

'There's no need. We're talking about taste, and we can't be held to account for our likes and dislikes. For what it's worth, I don't care particularly for the electric guitar, but I'm unlikely to be shot for saying that, at least if I stay away from Glastonbury and other potential trouble spots.'

When he'd heard the views of the rest of the class, he told them about their assignment.

'I want you to write a miniature, about twenty-four bars, for your least-favourite instrument. It can be witty, romantic, reflective, a lament or a celebration. I don't mind, but I do want you to demonstrate your awareness of the instrument's possibilities and limitations, and that's the point of this exercise: to experience the discipline of getting to know the instrument for which you're writing, whether you like it or not.'

Gavin had described the Rachmaninov sonata as 'climactic', and Leah couldn't disagree with that. After its brooding introduction, the tempo quickened and the excitement began, relaxing then into a new section that took her back by association to the previous Saturday night, thoughts of which she made a resolute effort to dispel, concentrating instead on listening to the music, which was as beautiful as Gavin had claimed. The cello playing was beautiful as well, although it impossible to separate from the piano part, so unified were the sonata and the ensemble.

The second movement afforded a relief after the ecstatic, surging music that had preceded it, and she enjoyed the exciting contrast of the racing arpeggios before the third movement took over, restful at first, and then swelling, flowing, rising and falling in a way that had become disturbingly familiar. Again, she concentrated on listening to the detail and seeing, in her imagination, the balletic possibilities of the piece.

The finale seemed to embody all the characteristics of the previous movements, leading the sonata to a breathless and dramatic ending, by which time Leah was convinced that, if ever a man understood anything of the female sexual experience, that man was Sergei Rachmaninov. She wanted to hear more of his music, although not immediately, as she doubted her ability to cope with it.

Afterwards, Gavin and the cellist were surrounded by excited students. Eventually, the admiring crowd broke up to go to its various lessons and lectures, and Leah could speak to Gavin.

'Oh, Gavin,' she said, 'congratulations. That was magnificent.'

'Thank you. I take it you're now a fan of Rachmaninov.'

'Oh, yes.' She inflected the words with a wealth of feeling.

He laughed. 'He evidently made a big impression.'

'It's a bit public here, Gavin. I'll tell you about it later.'

'How about tomorrow evening? I'm a hopeless cook, but we can go to a restaurant.'

'Can we make it Saturday? Friday's a bit cluttered with the late finish here, and it's nice to relax properly.'

'Agreed.'

'I must go. Congratulations again.'

22

It seemed to Leah that there was a conviviality about Italian restaurants generally, that was special and of a particular kind. It came possibly from a combination of the mixed aromas that emanated from the kitchen, and the outgoing, high-spirits of the Italian waiters. At all events, she felt she would never tire of it.

'That was wonderful,' she said, laying down her knife and fork with a sigh of contentment.

Gavin asked, 'As I'm driving, would you like to finish the wine? There's less than a glassful.'

'Are you trying to get me drunk?'

'Well, I have to use the tactics and devices available to me.' He poured the last of the wine into her glass.

'Just play Rachmaninov to me,' she said meaningfully, 'and I'm guaranteed to be a push-over.'

He smiled at the thought, and said, 'Sergei Vasilyevich must have eased the path of many a struggling lover.'

'Was that his name?'

'Sergei Vasilyevich Rachmaninov, yes. I'm told he once tried writing his name in the snow, as the other boys did, but he never quite reached the end.'

'Boys will be boys, they say.' She passed over the subject and said, 'I don't know of any ballet music by him. Do you?'

'I'm not aware that he ever wrote a ballet. If he did, the manuscript must have been lost.'

'I don't think he did, but ballets have been set to his music; The Symphonic Dances, for instance, although they've never appealed to me as much as the sonata did on Thursday.'

A waiter came to ask, 'Would you like to see the *dolce* trolley?'

Gavin looked at Leah, who shook her head. 'I couldn't eat another thing.'

'No, thank you,' Gavin told him. 'Just the bill, please.'

'I hope you enjoyed your meal, *signor e signorina*.'

'We did, thank you. It was excellent.'

'I bring your bill, *signor*.'

Leah watched him go, and said, 'We English are very stuffy compared with Italians. They really get to grips with life, somehow, whereas we seem to stand back and let things happen. My dad says the camp guards in Italy were mercurial and capricious, whereas the Germans tended to be cold and two-dimensional. A bit like us, really.'

'But Poland's a cold country, isn't it?'

'If it comes to that, Veano's in the north of Italy, right next to Switzerland. My dad and my Uncle Len tried to escape into Switzerland after the Italians walked away, but the Germans arrived and spoiled the party.'

'Their generation experienced so much.'

The thought was interrupted when the waiter arrived with the bill on a silver plate.

'Thank you. I'll pay that now.' He took out his wallet and counted the money plus a tip on to the plate.

'*Grazie, signor*. I bring your coats.'

Leah asked, 'What did your dad do in the war? You never talk about him.'

'That's because he wasn't around long enough for us to get to know him. He was in the RAF, apparently, but I'll be surprised if he didn't desert them as well. No, the hero at our house is Uncle Stan, a better man by far.' Recalling the original question, he said, 'Uncle Stan was a radio officer in the Merchant Navy. Atlantic convoys and then Russian convoys. He was torpedoed twice.'

Leah screwed her eyes up in horror. 'Poor man.'

'And he couldn't swim. It was a good thing they had lifejackets.'

'You're very fond of him, aren't you?'

'We all are. He has a big heart. He and my mum never married, and I don't know why, but he's filled the role in every other way. At least, I imagine he has.' He took Leah's coat from the waiter and helped her put it on.

When they reached Gavin's car, he patted it affectionately before opening the door for Leah.

She said, 'I feel like a gooseberry when I get into your car. I'd hate to come between the two of you.' She shivered at the coldness of the seat.

He asked, 'Are you wearing anything under that dress?'

'Of course,' she said, trying to sound affronted. 'How could you think otherwise?'

'I was thinking of last Saturday. When you took your dress off, you were topless and knickerless.'

'Oh, that. I'd just dropped my pants in the washing basket and I wasn't wearing a bra. When you have as little as I have, you don't always bother with one, and double "A"s are hard to find, anyway.'

Gavin negotiated the roundabout before saying, 'I think you're being unkind to them.'

'They know how I feel. Anyway, don't tell me you prefer flat-chested women, because I don't believe you.'

'No, I shan't tell you that. If I did, I'd be implying that I like flat-chested women generally, and I don't. My geography teacher had a chest like an ironing board – if she wore a tight dress on a cold day, she looked as if she was smuggling dried peas – and I couldn't stand her. All I'm saying is that I like you, and your boobs come with you as standard equipment, so I like them as well.'

'In that case, I find you not guilty.'

He pulled on to the crown of the road and waited for a gap in the oncoming traffic. 'Actually,' he said, 'I'm quite peeved that you accused me of being insincere.'

'Surely not.' She looked at him anxiously, and then saw a flicker of a smile. 'Just for a minute,' she said, 'I thought you were serious.'

'I am, and when we reach your place, I'm going to exact a penalty.'

'I can hardly wait.'

'Be careful what you wish for. This could be very different from what you have in mind.' He made the right turn into the lane that led to Leah's cottage.

'Please don't tell me we're going to do it with the light on,' she pleaded. 'I don't think I'm ready for that.'

'No, it's not that. Do you possess a Russian peasant's costume?'

'Doesn't everyone? Unfortunately, mine's in the wash. Every man I've slept with this week has insisted I wore it.'

'Don't worry. We can improvise.' He pulled in beside the cottage.

She asked, 'What are you going to wear?'

'Evening dress.'

'White tie and tails?'

'Of course. I'm going to be Rachmaninov and you'll be the woman who comes round to clean his *dacha*.'

'His what-cha?'

'His *dacha*, his country house. It was before he left Russia to live in America.' He got out to open the passenger door.

'What can I say? I'm waiting, all of a tremble, with me Hoover in me hand.'

'The vacuum cleaner hadn't been invented then.'

She unlocked the cottage door and opened it. 'Don't tell me you're one of those directors who insist on complete authenticity,' she said, closing the door after him. 'By the way, would you like a night cap?'

'No, thank you. Rachmaninov usually wore one of those tweed country hats, or a homberg when he visited the city.'

She took off her coat and hung it by the door. 'I meant a drink.'

'No, thanks. I never drink out of a hat.'

'In that case,' she said, kissing him seductively, 'come with me.' She led the way upstairs, leaving him, for the moment, in the bedroom.

When she returned, she found him examining the record she'd left on the lid of the turntable.

'The Rachmaninov Sonata,' he observed.

'Yes, I thought we could try it out.'

'In what sense?'

'As music to bonk to, of course.' She pulled her dress over her head and showed him that she was wearing at least one item of underwear. 'See?'

'I've never heard it called that,' he said, 'and yes, I see you're respectable.'

'Not now, I'm not.' She stepped out of the remaining garment. 'Haven't you heard of bonking? The students call it that.'

'Well, we live and learn, and it's a place of education, after all.'

'Gavin, please put the record on and get undressed. I'm feeling lonely.'

He shed the last of his clothes to join her just as a little-known Russian pianist and an equally obscure cellist eased their way into the Rachmaninov sonata.

She snuggled up to him, kissing him. 'You bugger,' she said, 'you kept me waiting on purpose.'

'Would I do a thing like that?' He kissed her and then addressed her breasts, kissing each of them elaborately and telling them, 'Whatever your owner says, I think you're both exquisite.'

'I don't think they're listening. At all events, they seem to have disappeared.' Reaching up, she switched off the light. 'There,' she said, 'now you'll never find them.'

'I can always find them,' he said, greeting them again.

She gave a shudder. 'I do believe you can.'

They played and teased for a while before eventually joining each other in blissful tandem. All the time, the music formed the perfect background, at least for Leah. She had no way of knowing how it affected Gavin, but it was natural for her to move when she heard music, and she did it quite unconsciously, until she became aware of a burgeoning sensation that was completely beyond her control. A great force was building up inside her and demanding to be released, although she had no idea how, and she was almost fearful of its growing strength. Then, suddenly, it was as if all her muscles had flown into reverse, and the force was released, flying from the centre of her body to its extremities, taking with it an irresistible, surging wave of warmth that left her gasping.

23

No one with any insight into Leah's personality could call her at all self-obsessed, but she continued to wonder until Monday morning about her happening at the weekend. Orgasm was no new experience for her, but she had never encountered it on that scale. Naturally enough, she wasn't going to complain, but the incident intrigued her nonetheless.

By nine-thirty, she decided that so much self-analysis was quite enough for one day, and she walked across to Vincent's office to find out if Neil had made any progress with the last act. As usual, she found Clare's office door open.

'Good morning, Clare.'

'Good morning, Leah. How can I help you?'

'Is Vincent in?'

'He's got a student with him. She's behind with her coursework, apparently.'

'Ah.' Leah had an idea who the student was. She tried another route. 'Has Neil given you any typing this morning? A script perhaps?'

'No. Sorry, Leah. Nothing at all.'

'Hell. That's okay, Clare. It's not your fault.'

Clare looked up at the clock. 'There's time yet. It's only just gone half-past. He may be teaching for all I know.'

How like Clare it was to make excuses for him. 'No, he's not teaching. I'll catch up with him later. Thanks, Clare.' She left the office and was about to return to hers, when she noticed someone sitting on the low wall by the carpark, where she had sat in September when she was waiting for her mother to pick her up. She couldn't see from that distance whether the student was male or female, but he or she seemed to be in acute distress.

As she hurried across, she recognised one of the male students from the Drama and Dance School. His name was Shaun Perry and he was sobbing uncontrollably.

'What's the matter, Shaun?'

He looked up and recognised her, but he was clearly unable to speak coherently.

'Come to my office. You'll be more comfortable there.'

He made no response, but continued to sob.

'We can have a coffee and a chat. Come on, Shaun.'

Gradually, he detached himself from the wall and followed her to her office.

'What do you like? Tea or coffee?' In the absence of a reply, she asked, 'Is coffee okay? That's what I'm having.'

He nodded, sniffing copiously. Leah passed him a box of tissues and busied herself with the coffee.

'Milk and sugar?'

He nodded. 'Three... sugars.' It was progress of a kind.

'There you are, Shaun.' She put a mug of coffee in front of him. 'Just the way your mum makes it, I hope. Take your time and then tell me what's troubling you.'

His eyes were filling with tears again.

'Who's your personal tutor, Shaun?'

He blurted out, 'Neil.'

Leah looked at her watch. Neil could be anywhere on the site. She asked, 'Have you spoken to him about your problem?' It was a fair question, because, had she been a student, she wouldn't have consulted Neil about the time of the next bus.

'It's all his... fault.'

'Neil's fault?'

'I really thought... he cared.' His breath was interrupted by shudders.

'Cared about what, Shaun?'

'About me.' He said it as if it should have been obvious.

'I imagine he cares about all his students.' She didn't really believe that, but it wasn't a good idea to let her doubt become known.

'You don't... understand. I thought he... fancied me.'

161

Things were falling into place now. 'Did you want him to fancy you, Shaun?'

'Of course I did. I really... thought....' He broke down again and sobbed.

Leah got up and put her hand on his shoulder, stroking him. It was against all the accepted advice, but the poor boy was distraught.

After some time, she spoke to him again. 'Shaun,' she said, 'what did Neil do to make you think he fancied you?'

'It was... just the way he... spoke to me. It felt like the real thing.'

'Did he touch you at all?'

'No, he just... has that way... of speaking and... looking at me.'

She could imagine that. It was what she'd feared for some time. She picked up the internal phone and dialled Vincent's number. It rang twice and he answered.

'Vincent.'

'Vincent, it's Leah. Are you terribly busy just now?'

'Not if it's important. What's the matter, Leah?'

'I have a very distressed student in my office. It's a sensitive matter. Can you come over?'

'Of course.'

Leah put the phone down. 'Shaun,' she said, 'how long have you known you were gay?'

'Years. Three or four years.'

'You see, it's important for you to know that Neil's not gay.'

Shaun stared at her in disbelief. 'You're wrong,' he said. 'He is. I can tell.'

There was a knock on the door and Vincent walked in.

'Shaun,' she said, 'hand on heart, Neil's not gay. You must have read signs that weren't there.'

He burst into a fresh outpouring of tears, and Leah turned to Vincent to say, 'Shaun was convinced that Neil felt the same way about him, and now, somehow, he's discovered that wasn't the case. He's told me that Neil hasn't touched him at any time, but he's looked at him and spoken to him in a way that seemed to suggest affection.'

Vincent spoke to Shaun for the first time. 'Shaun,' he said, 'what are your feelings towards Neil?'

162

'I... I really fancy him a lot, and I thought he....'

'Yes, I understand that, but what Leah's told you is true. Neil is not gay. You must have misread him.'

'No.' The protest was almost a wail. 'He kept... giving me the... come-on, and then... he told me I'd got... the wrong idea.'

'When did he tell you that?'

'This morning.'

'Listen, Shaun,' said Vincent. 'I want you to stay here in Leah's office until you're more collected. I'm going to speak to Neil about this, and then I may need to speak to you again. Do you understand?'

'Yes.'

Vincent motioned Leah to follow him to the door. When they were out of earshot, he said, 'There's just a chance I can deal with this without the Principal having to know about it.' He consulted his watch. 'What are your movements this morning?'

'I've got nothing until eleven, and then I have a dance class.'

'All right. I'm going to find Neil now, and then I'll come for Shaun. Do you mind keeping an eye on him until I'm ready for him?'

'Not at all.'

'Thank you, Leah. I'll see you later.'

Vincent collected Shaun at a little after ten-thirty, so Leah was able to leave in good time for her class. On her way, she saw Neil. He was about to enter his office when he turned and saw her.

'I've just been roasted alive,' he said. His tone was resentful.

'Well, it serves you bloody-well right.' She said no more, but continued to the dance studio.

She had a useful session with the second-year students, during which she gave the Shaun situation barely a thought. On leaving the dance studio, however, she almost collided with Vincent.

'Oh, Leah,' he said, 'have you seen Shaun recently?'

'Not since you called for him. What's happened?'

'I left him in my office for five minutes, and when I returned, he'd gone. I waited, in case he'd just nipped out to the loo, but there was no sign of him.'

Leah tried to think of places where he might have gone. 'Could he be in the Refectory or the Students' Union, do you think?'

'I've checked them both. No one there has seen him either.'

'Could he have gone back to his lodgings?'

'He's local. He lives at home in Bishop Monckton.'

Leah thought quickly. 'Has he got his own transport?'

'Yes, a Lambretta, apparently.'

'There must be a few of them in the carpark, but the registration should be on file.'

'Good thinking.' He turned towards Clare's office. 'You keep a look out for him while I get the number.'

Leah kept watch, thankful, in the cold wind, that she hadn't changed into a leotard and tights for the class. Eventually, Vincent returned with a scrap of paper.

'Got it,' he said. 'Let's look in the carpark.'

They hurried across the asphalted area to the low wall where Leah had found Shaun earlier. Leah asked, 'What's the number, Vincent?'

He showed her the piece of paper, and she read the registration EUM 844H.

'It's a blue-and-white Lambretta,' he told her.

They searched the whole of the carpark without success.

'I'll give him half-an-hour,' said Vincent, 'and then I'll phone his home.'

'It's all you can do,' said Leah.

'I shouldn't tell you this, Leah, but Neil is quite unrepentant. He can't see that he's done anything at all wrong. I've reminded him repeatedly that these students are vulnerable and impressionable, but he seems incapable of responsible thought.'

'With an ego like his, responsibility is an alien concept.'

'Oh, well.' Vincent looked at his watch. 'There's no reason why this business should disrupt any more of your day, Leah. Leave it with me and I'll let you know when anything happens.'

She found Gavin in the café. He was about to order, so she took a quick look at the menu and made a decision. 'What are you having?'

'Why do women always ask that question?' He turned to the waitress and said, 'I'd like the quiche Lorraine salad, please.'

'The same for me, please,' said Leah, 'and we'd like a cafetiere of coffee for two.'

When the waitress was gone, Leah asked, 'Are you turning over a new leaf?'

'No, I just like the quiche-thing.'

'It's the salad that's the surprise, although it's not the only surprise today.' She told him about Shaun and about Vincent's involvement.

'Poor little bugger,' said Gavin. 'Shaun, I mean.'

'Yes, although it's possibly an unfortunate word to use in this case.'

'I mean, with the best intentions, I still find their world a strange and unnatural one, but that doesn't make it less hurtful for the poor little sod.'

'I agree, and I imagine "sod" was a slip of the tongue.'

'Thank you. And you say he's disappeared into thin air?'

'Apparently. Vincent was going to try phoning his home later, to see if he's arrived.' She shook her head. 'I must say, this kind of thing's no good for Shaun or for the other students.'

'In medieval times, they'd have strung Neil up by his wedding tackle.'

'Shaun as well, unfortunately. They weren't too particular in those days.' After some reflection, she said, 'Maybe I was a bit abrupt when I told Shaun that Neil was straight.'

'Why do you think that?'

'His reaction. It was as if I'd told him the earth was square.'

Gavin put his hand on hers and stroked it with his thumb. 'He was bound to react sharply. He had a big crush on Neil, and suddenly his dream was shattered.'

'You're probably right.' She managed a smile on the strength of it. 'It feels good,' she said. 'I can talk to you about these things.'

'You said you had to know a man well before you could trust him. Have I passed the test?'

'Yes, I give you "A-plus", and that's possibly the answer to a mystery.'

He was instantly curious. 'Do tell.'

'On Saturday night,' she said, 'I got quite excited.'

'I can't disagree with that. At one stage, I thought you were going to shake the plaster off the ceiling.'

'It's never affected me as dramatically as that. It was a surprise, to say the least, and I don't think Rachmaninov was solely responsible.'

Gavin waited while the waitress set down their quiches and coffee. When they were alone, he returned to the conversation. 'Maybe Rachmaninov helped to some extent, but do you think,' he said, 'it was because you were more relaxed than you've been in times past?'

'I think you've hit the nail on the head,' she said confidently, 'and that observation alone makes you stand out from the crowd. A lot of men would have put it down to superior cocksmanship.'

Feigning guilt, he said, 'The thought did cross my mind, but modesty prevailed.'

Vincent's efforts to contact Shaun continued without success, until the following morning.

When Leah arrived, he was waiting for her, and she could tell from his air of concern that something was badly wrong.

'I've just spoken to Shaun's mother,' he said. 'She'd been at the hospital last evening and most of the night. It seems that when he got home, he helped himself to her sleeping pills. When she got in from work, she went to his room to pick up his laundry, and she found him unconscious.'

24

'They pumped out the contents of his stomach,' said Vincent, 'and he's conscious again. His mother had gone home to pick up his sponge bag and things, so it was lucky I caught her. That's if "lucky" is the word.'

'What did you tell her? I mean, about why he'd gone home.'

'I told her the truth, Leah. I owed her that, at the very least.'

'So the cat's out of the bag.' Leah considered the implications. 'Mind you,' she said, 'if we have a problem, Shaun and his mum have a much greater one. Is there a Mr Perry?'

'Yes, somewhere, not living with them. Mrs Perry is the active parent, and she knew Shaun had something on his mind. He's often spoken to her about Neil, and she was afraid it might be developing into an unhealthy crush. She knows Shaun's gay, by the way.'

'That's one adjustment she doesn't have to make.'

'No, and it's early days yet, but I think she's being remarkably philosophical.'

'She must be a remarkable woman,' observed Leah. Then, as one thought led to the next, she asked, 'Does Neil know yet?'

'I'm waiting for him to arrive,' said Vincent grimly.

'In that case, I'll leave you to it. I have to see Gavin about something.'

She walked up the sloping driveway to the Music School, envying its staff, not for the first time, their lawns and flower beds. She exchanged a cheery greeting with Maggie, the Head of School's secretary, and continued to Gavin's office, reasonably confident he'd be there, knowing how he felt about the Common Room.

She knocked, as courtesy demanded, and received the invitation to enter.

'Good morning, Leah.'

'Good morning, Gavin.' She closed the door and favoured him with a discreet kiss. 'Have you finished the music for the Attendant Spirits?'

'I worked on it through the night.'

'Surely not.'

'We'll, I finished at about two o'clock.'

'You're a one-off, Gavin.' She took the manuscript from him. 'Is there any news about Shaun Perry?'

'Yes, he tried to end his misery last night with his mum's sleeping tablets.'

'Oh, no. Poor little bug... soul.'

'He's conscious again. They pumped it all out at the hospital.'

'Thank God for that. Does Neil know?'

'I imagine he'll have arrived by now, and Vincent will have told him.'

'It'll be interesting to see how long it is before he tries playing the victim.'

'My money says he'll have tried it already. Anyway, I mustn't linger.'

'Here's something to take with you.' He handed her a tape cassette.

She looked at the title, which was in his handwriting. It said, *Colloquio en la reja – Enrique Granados.* 'Did you record this?'

'Yes, on the Steinway in the Recital Hall. I thought it might appeal to you. If you find Rachmaninov's music erotic, just try that for size.'

'She looked again at the title, and asked, 'What does it mean? I don't speak Spanish.'

' "Conversation Over the Fence", as between lovers, that is. It's a sort of love duet.'

'Oh, I'll look forward to that.' Then, she remembered her other reason for calling. 'By the way,' she said, 'I shan't be around at the weekend. I have to go home. My mum has to have an operation. She's going in on Friday.'

'Nothing awful, I hope.'

'It's major but routine. She's having a hysterectomy.'

'Come again?'

'They're removing her womb,' she explained.

'Ah, I've heard of that. I see what you mean by "major", but it is fairly routine, isn't it?'

'That's what I keep telling myself.'

'I mean, lots of women must have it done. They just don't talk about it much. Give her my best wishes, won't you? In fact, if you give me the name of the hospital, I'll send her some flowers.'

'Oh, Gavin, that's really sweet of you. Look, I really must go, but I'll see you before the weekend, naturally. Thanks for the tape.' She heard footsteps on the corridor, and played safe by blowing a kiss.

They saw each other the next morning when they arrived for a hastily-called meeting with Vincent.

'I'm sorry to bring you both here at such short notice,' he said, 'but things have reached a watershed. The fact is, Neil phoned in sick this morning. His doctor has signed him off, initially for a month, although it could easily be for longer.'

Leah was the first to speak. 'Is this illness coincidental or irresponsible-pillock-related?'

'Depression,' confirmed Vincent, 'following the shock news about Shaun Perry.'

'Have you heard how Shaun is?'

'Yes, he's had an awful time, he's now highly relieved that his suicide attempt was unsuccessful, and he could be back with us before very long.'

'That's good news.'

'It is,' agreed Gavin.

'However,' said Vincent, 'Neil's absence leaves us with a problem. Between us, the Drama staff and I will take on his teaching load, but then we have to consider the play.' He looked at them both and said, 'Unless either of you has any objection, I'll write the final scene and take over as director.'

'It's a lot of work for you, Vincent,' said Gavin, 'but I can't see any alternative.'

'There's no one else capable of doing it,' agreed Leah.

'So we're agreed on that.' Vincent patted the script and went on. 'It's necessary to decide who wins the election to the Upper Chambers, and I think that's best done by the three of us. What I suggest is that we do it by binning the obvious suspects and then prioritising the rest, rather as in a balloon debate.'

'Good idea,' said Leah.

'Yes,' said Gavin, 'it makes sense.'

'Right, let's go through the *Dramatis Personae*.' He took the relevant page from the script and began. 'I think we can discount the Tsars and Tsarinas of Russia, Ivan the Terrible, Catherine the Great, Henry the Eighth, King John, Mary Tudor, Philip of Spain and Kaiser Wilhelm the Second. Are there any others?'

There was silence as they considered the question, and then Leah asked, 'How do we feel about Edward the Eighth? There was a degree of sympathy towards him and Wallis Simpson.'

'As I see it,' said Gavin, 'he dodged the column and left the responsibility as an unwelcome surprise for his brother.'

'Okay,' said Vincent, 'let's bin him as well. What about Good Queen Bess?'

'Too many executions,' said Leah. 'When she was good, she was very, very good, but she had her off-with-his-head-days.'

'Right, let's bin her. Anyone else?'

'Queen Victoria,' suggested Leah, but without real conviction.

Vincent shook his head. 'I don't think so. She shut herself away after Albert died, and ignored all calls for her to resume public life.' He picked up the list again. 'Okay, let's see who's left. There's Albert the First of Belgium, Wilhelmina of the Netherlands, Gustavus Adolphus of Sweden, Lady Jane Grey, Richard the Lionheart, Henry the Seventh, Charles the Second, William and Mary, George the Fifth, George the Sixth, Boadicea, Edward the Seventh, Wilhelm the First and, of course, the Caesars of Rome.'

Leah and Gavin consulted their copies. Gavin said, 'I know Richard the Lionheart pursued a good cause, but he neglected his country and allowed his unspeakable brother far too much licence.'

'Agreed,' said Vincent. 'Let's bin him.'

'Leah asked, 'What about William and Mary, or either of them, the first constitutional monarchs?'

'No,' said Vincent. 'Much of the trouble we're experiencing in Northern Ireland is down to them.' He looked again at his list and said, 'While we're about it, I think we should bin the Caesars of Rome.'

There were nods of agreement. Leah said, 'No one's perfect. Most of them have skeletons in their cupboards.'

'George the Sixth stands up well,' said Gavin. 'He took the job on when his brother did a bunk, and then he and the Queen Mother stayed with their people in London throughout the Blitz. That makes him a hero in my eyes.'

'He's an excellent candidate, but for two things,' said Vincent. 'He's too shy to put himself forward, and he's not at all ambitious, just content to wait for Elizabeth to join him.'

'It's a shame.'

'Just a minute,' said Leah. 'What about Lady Jane Grey? She was charming and clever, as I recall, and popular too. She reigned for just nine days and was deposed and put to death by that vicious old bat Bloody Mary.'

Vincent looked thoughtful. 'She was a reigning monarch. What do you say, Gavin?'

'I'll give her my vote. I'll have to write a song for her, but that's no task at all.'

'All those in favour.' Vincent added his hand to theirs. 'That's settled, then. Lady Jane Grey will be elected to the Upper Chambers. Thank you, both, for your help. I'll be in touch.'

As they left Vincent's office, Gavin said, 'You were right. Neil lost no time in casting himself as the victim.'

'That must have been quite a performance he put on for his doctor.' She inclined her head towards her office and asked, 'Have you time for a chat?'

He looked at his watch. 'I'm okay for half-an-hour or so.'

'I'll put the coffee on. I imagine Vincent was too caught up with events to think about it this morning.'

Gavin closed the office door behind him and took a seat. He asked, 'Has this thing come upon your mum very recently?'

'No, she's been affected by hot flushes and, without going into gory detail, the usual things associated with the menopause for some time. Her inside bits started misbehaving towards the end of last year. Fortunately, she has private health insurance, so she was able to see a specialist straight away, and he advised her to have the operation.' She passed a business card across the desk to him. 'That's the name and address of the hospital,' she said. 'It's where I had my last knee operation.'

'How many have you had?'

She counted on her fingers. 'Five.'

'Surely they've put it right by now.'

'I hope so. It's a mess in there,' she said, pointing to her knee.

'It must have been a terrible shock. The accident, I mean.'

'It was, but the second shock came in hospital, when they told me I'd be laid up for weeks and possibly months, and that they couldn't guarantee complete recovery. The were grooming me for success at the ballet school, you know. Everyone was looking forward to a bright future for me, and then an irresponsible driver came hurtling down Regent Street and changed that future in a split second.'

'I'm sorry.' He reached across the desk to stroke her hand.

'No, I'm the one who should be sorry, moaning about it after all this time.'

'When I was a kid,' he told her, 'my mum kept telling me to work hard at school like my brother Graham, because if I failed the eleven-plus, there'd be no future for me. She really believed that and, being young and naïve, so did I. Anyway, when the results were announced, and I learned that I'd failed, I was devastated.'

'That's awful.'

'Yes, and my mum told me to brace up. She said, "You're a big boy now, and big boys don't make a fuss." Now, it just happened that Uncle Stan was at home, and when he heard her say that, he said, "What's that? Big boys don't make a fuss? They do if it hurts badly enough." And the same applies to big girls, Leah, so moan if you want to. I don't mind.'

She clasped his hand, grateful for his sympathy. 'What happened then? Surely things weren't so bad at school.'

'It was great. We had teachers who cared about us, a brilliant music department, and I had the best clarinet teacher in the world, or so it seemed. Graham had a miserable time at the grammar school.'

'What about your piano teacher?'

'She was excellent too, but she taught me privately, thanks again to Uncle Stan.' He looked at his watch and said, 'I have to leave you.' He slipped the hospital card into his top pocket.

'Would you like to come over tonight?'

'Or you could come to my place.'

'Let's not get territorial. I'll cook for you.'

'I'm almost persuaded.'

'I've been listening to the Granados.' Sensuously, she half-closed her eyes. 'It was quite a surprise.'

'I'll come to your place.'

25

'She was still dopey after the anaesthetic last night.'

'She would be, Dad. She'll feel a lot better today.' Reassuring her parent was a new experience for Leah, a kind of role reversal, but she had to do it. 'When's Martin coming?'

'This afternoon.' He changed down to turn into the hospital car-park. 'He'll come straight here.'

'Oh, good.'

'He's been home quite a lot recently.'

'Oh, yes?'

'He's spending a lot of time with Wendy.'

'Good for him.'

He parked in the nearest place he could find to the entrance, as was his habit at supermarkets and dance venues, because it helped him find his car later. He had a history of forgetting where he'd parked.

'It's funny,' he said. 'We thought Wendy's interest in wildlife was a ploy to get in with Martin, but it turns out she really is keen.' He saw Leah smile, and said, 'Keen on nature, I mean.' He took the flowers from the back seat and locked the doors.

'Keen on both, I shouldn't wonder.'

'By the way, Bailey and Elaine have invited me to stay with them next weekend. It solves the messing problem and it'll be just as easy for me to get to the hospital.'

'Why do you call it "messing", Dad. You're not in the Navy now.'

'It's just a habit.'

She took his arm as they walked to the entrance, and she said, 'Gavin's uncle was in the merchant navy during the war, on Atlantic and Russian convoys. He was torpedoed twice.'

'Poor devil. The Med was bad enough, but to hell with ditching in icy-cold oggin.'

They came to a door not far from Leah's old room. 'Here we are,' announced her father, opening the door to announce their arrival.

'Oh, lovely.' Her mother greeted them weakly, although she was clearly delighted to see them , but she looked awful. She wore no make-up, which wasn't surprising, but she looked washed out, and Leah caught herself wondering if she, too, had looked like that after her operation. She waited while her father kissed her mother, and then went to the side of the bed. 'Hello, Mum.' She kissed her and then laid her cheek next to hers for comfort. 'How are you feeling?'

'Tired and sore, but all right, really.'

'You will feel sore after what they've done to you.' She kissed her again because she looked so pathetic.

'I left my make-up bag at home,' said her mum. 'I must look like the wreck of the Hesperus.'

'You'll never look like that,' Leah assured her, 'but I'll bring your make-up in next time I come.'

'You're a good girl, Leah, and you'll never guess what came today.'

Leah tried to think of something connected with her being a good girl, but failed. 'I give in,' she said. 'What came today?'

'I think your mum's talking about these.' Her father was pointing to a vase of flowers on the windowsill. 'They're from Gavin.' He handed the card to her.

'He said he'd send you some flowers.' She read the message and handed the card back to her father.

'Wasn't that kind of him?'

'Yes, Mum.'

'Do you see much of him nowadays?'

Leah was conscious that her dad was grinning to himself, but she ignored him. 'Yes,' she said, thankful that her mum didn't know just how much of Gavin she'd been seeing. 'We work together,' she reminded her.

'Of course. He's such a lovely young man, isn't he, Freddy?'

'Yes, I liked him.'

Leah sighed. Her mother would never be satisfied until she

knew. 'Gavin and I are now an item,' she said, 'but don't dash out to buy a hat. I mean, even when you're fit.'

'Oh, I'm so glad. Aren't you, Freddy?'

'Well, he's a big improvement on some of his predecessors. I think Leah's beginning to get the hang of it.'

'Freddy, behave yourself.'

When Leah looked round, her father was smiling.

'When's Martin coming?'

'This afternoon,' Leah told her.

'He's been home quite a lot lately.'

'Yes, I hear so.' She couldn't help saying, 'That's Wendy's influence, I expect.'

'As a matter of fact,' said her father, 'Wendy brought me a really nice ham salad for lunch yesterday. She knew I was alone and she took pity on me.'

'She has hidden qualities,' said Leah.

'Is that a "miaow"?'

'No, Dad, you know me better than that, and I think she'll be good for Martin.'

'But do leave them to get on with it,' said her mum.

'I shan't interfere. We all know that matchmaking is your department.' Leah bent and kissed her. 'Love you, Mum. Now, rest and get well again. I'm going to leave you two now.'

'I love you too, darling. Where are you going?'

'I'm going to see if I can find any of the staff who looked after me last summer.' Turning the door handle, she said, 'In any case, you need some time together.'

That afternoon, Leah made a beef stew that would feed her dad, Martin and herself that evening and leave enough for her dad to re-heat another day, although she suspected Wendy might have plans for later. Her inkling was confirmed when Wendy called in after work to ask after Leah's mum and to find out if there was any way she might be helpful.

'I hope you don't mind me doing things for your dad, Leah,' she said. 'You'll let me know if I'm treading on your toes, won't you?'

'Loud and clear, Wendy, but I'm very grateful for any help, and I'm sure my dad is too.'

'Good. Well, don't worry about him through the week. I'll see he gets something for a puttin' on and then a meal at night.' She looked as if something else had occurred to her, because she said, 'When your mum comes home, she'll have to take it easy, won't she? They always say no reaching, stretching, pushing, pulling and that sort of thing.'

'That's right.'

'Well, I'll be around to fetch and carry for her, and I'll do the hoovering and ironing as well, just as long as you don't mind.'

'Bless you, Wendy. You're very kind.'

'Well, we're neighbours, an' that's what it's all about. That's right, isn't it, Martin?'

Leah wasn't aware that Martin had joined them in the kitchen, until Wendy spoke to him. She turned to him and said, 'Wendy's going to look after Dad this week, Martin. That's kind of her, isn't it?'

'Yes, it is.'

Wendy looked at him as a mother might regard a child struggling with the complexities of social interaction, which, in effect, Martin was, despite his 22 years. 'You don't say much, do you, Martin? But you're nice to have around.' She pulled him towards her and kissed him.

'I think I'll leave you two alone,' said Leah. 'Two's company, an' all that.'

―――

She returned to her cottage on Sunday night, confident that her mum was recovering nicely, and that her dad was being well cared-for; in fact, the signs were that Wendy was about to smother him with attention. Her plans for Martin were abundantly clear, and he seemed happy enough for her to be around him.

―――

Now that the script was complete, Gavin had completed a song for Lady Jane Grey. It was the number with which she was to state her case to the Supreme Council, and his ignorance of her life and plight had led him to the Reference Department of the Public Library. He was fascinated by what he learned, and disappointed that he could use so little of it.

LADY JANE GREY:

I am the forgotten queen, once crowned but lost in history.
My fate is known, yet little else but myth suffused in mystery.
The English crown I never sought; the plot was false, nay, rotten.
The nearest heiress, Mary Tudor, true, if misbegotten.

And that because her mother's claim on Henry was made void,
Yet Mary was the rightful queen, the claimant unalloyed.
I pleaded thus, yet, heeded not, my cries found deafest ears,
And I was forced to ascend the throne, a queen at sixteen years.

CHAIRMAN [speaking]: *Who forced you, Jane?*
JANE: *My father, sir, though I am ashamed to say it, and my fa-ther-in-law, the Duke of Northumberland.*
CHAIRMAN: *What was their motive in this manoeuvring?*
JANE: *Mary, as you know, sir, was a Catholic, and my family would own but a Protestant monarch. To this end, my father-in-law per-suaded His Majesty King Edward the Sixth to declare me his successor.*
CHAIRMAN: *Thank you, Jane. Please continue with your testimony.*

JANE [sings]: *A life of sport and pastime held no appeal for me,*
To ultimate enlightenment was scholarship the key,
Socrates and Plato I longed to introduce,
To a nation starved of culture, made rotten by abuse.

In my childlike purpose, I would see myself erase,
The state of moral poverty that men would fain embrace.
With will, such deeds would flourish in time, and with goodwill,
But time was then denied me, and kindness was there nil.

There was further questioning, culminating in Jane's simple statement, forgiving Mary Tudor.

Gavin could find no evidence of Jane's desire to foster learning, but it was a popular myth, and the show needed a sympathetic character to triumph at the end.

26

APRIL

Leah arrived in time for the lunch-hour recital. 'Shaun's back in college,' she said.

'Good.'

'Yes.' She looked at her programme and said, 'I'd no idea what was happening today,' she said. 'I just thought I'd take potluck.'

'It's one of my students. He's playing a sonata by Beethoven.' Gavin felt obliged to add, 'It's not at all erotic. Beethoven lived alone and, as far as we know, had only one, unsuccessful, relationship with a woman.'

'It was hardly worth my coming, then.'

'Not in the least. He wrote superb music.'

'I know.' She smiled. 'Only kidding.' She looked again at her programme and said, 'So it's not like the Erotica Symphony?'

'Do you mean the *Eroica* Symphony?'

'Hey, you hear it your way and I'll hear it mine.'

They fell silent as Clive took his place at the piano. Sensibly, he was going to play from the printed score, and a fellow-student sat beside him to turn his pages. Gavin gave him a reassuring smile and then closed his eyes, because, however well Clive played, the next twenty minutes would seem like purgatory. His student was only a matter of yards away, but if things went wrong because of nerves or for any other reason, Gavin would be unable to help him. He listened to the *staccato* opening and hoped for the best.

There was a fluffed passage as Clive went into the second group of themes, but he kept going, and seemed to gather confidence, so that, by the end of the first movement, it was clear that he was enjoying the experience.

During the slow movement and the Minuet, Gavin was able to relax to some extent and enjoy the way his *protégé* was performing. With the last movement, marked *prestissimo*, however, he was once again in a limbo of tension that continued up to the concluding bars, when a plummeting arpeggio brought the music to its abrupt and dramatic end.

Relieved and delighted, Gavin joined in the applause.

'It's all over now,' Leah told him. 'You can breathe again.'

'Was it so obvious?'

'Not really, but I know what it's like. I go through torment for my students too.'

Next on the platform were two mature students, ex-armed-forces bandsmen, who performed Poulenc's Sonata for Two Clarinets, a work that proved too discordant and shrill for Leah's taste, because she kept her eyes and lips tightly closed throughout.

Afterwards, she said, 'That did nothing for me, but I'd like to offer my congratulations to your student.'

'Let's go and find him,' suggested Gavin.

They found Clive enjoying the felicitations of his fellow-students, who made way for Gavin and Leah.

'Well played, Clive,' said Gavin, shaking his hand. 'This is Leah from Dance and Drama. She was impressed too.'

'That was excellent, Clive,' said Leah, also shaking his hand.

'Thank you. I'm afraid I hit some bum notes in the first movement.'

'Did you?' Gavin looked surprised. 'I wasn't aware of any.'

'Well done, Clive.' The voice came from behind Gavin, but he recognised it as that of Paul Bright.

'Thank you, Mr Bright.'

Gavin watched his colleague recede into the distance, and remarked, 'You were always safe with Beethoven, Clive. Only the most dedicated Early Music purist could find his music vulgar or vacuous.'

Afterwards, Leah asked him, 'What was that about vacuous music?'

'Just a bit of intra-school backbiting.'

'Oh, do you get it here as well?'

'By the bucketful.'

As they walked back to Leah's office, she said, 'At this late stage, I've had some thoughts about the final scene, about Lady Jane's supplication.'

'Have you?' He hadn't envisaged dance being part of it, but it would be interesting to hear her idea.

'When she's telling her story to the Supreme Council, I suggest an enactment in ballet, of her execution. I think it would stop just short of the beheading. Of course, to make it suitably distant, it would take place behind a gauze screen. What do you think?'

'It sounds like a good idea. I think it would emphasise the tragedy before the happy ending. Have you put it to Vincent?'

'Not yet. I'm seeing him this afternoon. I need to talk to him about the dance presentation.' She opened her office door to let him in.

'What dance presentation?'

'The Third Year final. They're dancing a sequence from *Giselle*.'

'Oh, can I come and watch?'

'I'm afraid it's a private showing for the external assessors. Otherwise, you'd have been welcome.' She sat behind her desk and asked, 'How's the orchestra coming along?'

'Slowly and a trifle unsurely, but they'll get there. I think I did the right thing in keeping it small.'

'How small?'

'Nineteen players. It should be all right. The Thomas Arne is quite a small theatre, as I recall, but big enough for our production.' Memories of what Freddy and Sylvia had achieved in Easingthorpe's modest Town Hall reminded him to ask, 'How's your mum?'

'Much better, thanks. Wendy's been helping her with the things she hasn't to do, the jobs that use the abdominal muscles, so she's recovering nicely. She's coming to the show.'

'Good. Who else is coming?'

Counting unnecessarily on her fingers, as was her custom, Leah recited, 'My dad, obviously, Martin, Wendy, Bailey, Elaine and Janice. You know, I could almost envy those students, singing and dancing in a London theatre. It's something I never did.' She seemed to make a conscious effort to put that thought behind her, and said, 'Who are you bringing?'

'My mum, Uncle Stan, Graham and Frank Morrison. I'm still trying to get hold of Hutch and Ellie.'

'Who?'

'My clarinet teacher and his wife.'

'After all the effort he put in, training you up to be a gentleman, I hope you manage to find him. It's good that Frank's coming as well. What's Hutch's wife like?'

'Quite ladylike; her father was big in worsted spinning, but I always found her kind and affectionate. I've always been fond of her.'

'Did she fill a place in your life?'

'She did. My mum had to be tough, bringing up two kids alone, at least for a while, and she expected us to be as tough, hence the eleven-plus thing I told you about. On the other hand, Ellie was like a favourite auntie, the kind that spoils you rotten if they're allowed. She and Hutch were – in fact, still are – special people to Frank and Penny and me.'

'In that case, let's hope our show lives up to their expectations.'

Forty miles away, Wendy was on her lunch break and, as usual, called on Freddy and Sylvia to see if they needed any shopping.

'Not a thing, Wendy,' said Sylvia, 'but thank you for coming. You don't know what it means to us.'

'We're neighbours,' said Wendy, as if that meant everything, and it seemed to, as far as she was concerned.

'Well, I've got something for you,' said Freddy, handing her a leather case.

'Oh, what's this?' She seemed almost afraid to touch it.

'Open it and find out,' he suggested.

She unbuckled the single strap to open the case and gasped as she drew out its contents. 'Ross binoculars, like Martin's,' she breathed.

'Take them and enjoy them, Wendy.'

'But they must have cost a fortune,' she said, turning towards the window and focusing them on a house at the end of the street.

'Not quite that. They were old stock, not made any longer. In any case, it's little enough after all you've done for us.'

'Thank you, Freddy. They're lovely.' She placed them carefully in their case and fastened it. 'Is it all right for me to give him a kiss, Sylvia?'

'Oh, I think I can allow that.'

Wendy leaned forward to kiss Freddy on the cheek, and then did the same to Sylvia. 'Fair shares,' she said. 'Anyway, I have to go. Thanks again, Freddy.'

When she was gone, Sylvia said, 'That girl is kindness on legs.'

'Yes,' said Freddy, 'her legs are special too.' His remark earned him a playful slap on the wrist.

Changing the subject, Sylvia said, 'I really don't know what to expect with this show we're going to. It sounds very peculiar.'

'It's certainly different,' agreed Freddy. 'Let's just go and enjoy it.'

Two weeks later, Gavin was rehearsing the orchestra for the show.

'Right, we'll leave the overture for the time being. Michael's here,' he said, pointing out a student who had just joined them. 'He's playing King Edward the Seventh, and I'd like us to go through his number.'

Two guitarists and a banjo player tuned their instruments in readiness, and Michael left his seat to sing the number.

The first guitarist played a loud chord.

'I was a prince for sixty years, the envy of my peers,
Though the benefit was hard to recognise.'

His accent was spot-on, and he knew the song well. The first verse began, and Gavin relaxed, giving only a metronomic beat as the song went on. It was self-indulgence, and it was a shame when it had to end.

'Thank you, Michael. That was excellent.' Turning to the guitarists and banjo player, he said, 'Thank you, also, Carl, Patrick and

Alan. You were also excellent. It's going to be a popular number.' Turning again to look behind him, he saw Leah and half-a-dozen students, one of whom he recognised as the girl playing Lady Jane Grey.

'We're going to rehearse a number from the final act,' he told the orchestra. This is where Lady Jane pleads her case to the Council and, as she does so, her execution is enacted by dancers. They'll do it behind gauze on the night. Are you ready, Jane and the dancers? Jane, you have just two bars of intro and you're in with "I am the forgotten queen".'

'Right, Gavin.'

'If everyone's ready, we'll begin.'

The orchestra played the introduction, and Lady Jane began.

'I am the forgotten queen, once crowned but lost in history.' She had the perfect voice for the part, with little *vibrato* and seemingly artless, and she sang and enunciated he song well.

After the first two verses, Leah read the part of the Chairman in the dialogue, after which Jane returned to her song, ending with, 'But time was then denied me, and kindness was there nil.' It was the cue for the ballet, and as Jane knelt in supplication, the dancers performed her earthly end, the girl dancing the part of Jane giving an excellent performance. Then, Leah read the lines of the Chairman again as the strings of the orchestra provided a *pianissimo* background.

'Why was it so important for you to instruct the nation, Jane?'

The dialogue continued until Jane's announcement of forgiveness, and then Gavin brought up the volume for the dramatic final four bars.

As he cut the orchestra off, he said, 'Absolutely well done, everyone.'

'Yes,' agreed Leah, 'that was excellent.'

Gavin closed his score and gave the orchestra the 'thumbs up' sign. 'That is a powerful scene,' he said. 'Okay, thank you, everyone. The same time tomorrow, please.' He watched the dancers go, and asked Leah, 'Where did you find the girl who's dancing Jane?'

'Dawn? She's our secret weapon. I'm resting her until that scene.'

'How do you think it's going so far?'

Leah touched the wooden rostrum as she said, 'So far, so good.'

'Do you fancy a drink?'

'Wouldn't you prefer one at the cottage?'

'If I can pick up some things from my place as we go, I really think I should.'

~⚮~

Much later, they lay together listening to the unaccustomed rain on the window.

'Thank goodness for that,' said Leah. 'I thought it had forgotten how to rain.'

'The cricket season's almost upon us,' Gavin remarked wistfully.

'Are you keen on cricket?'

'Yes, I played for my school until my piano teacher found out.'

'Oh, wasn't she impressed?'

'She went bananas. She said, "Just break one finger and you'll never be a concert pianist." '

Leah studied his hands. Finally, she selected a finger with a crooked joint, and asked, 'Did you break this one?'

'Yes.'

'Is that why you're not a concert pianist?'

'No, I just never made the grade.'

'But you're brilliant.'

'Thank you. Still, it takes tremendous ability to make a living at it, and that's not me, I'm afraid. I've given recitals from time to time, but I'll never be famous.'

'When I knew I was never going to be a dancer,' she said, snuggling up to him, 'I wondered what I could do instead.'

'What did you consider?'

She giggled. 'The usual things: pantomime, juggling, ventriloquism, impressions, conjuring…. I might have been good at that. I mean, I can make two things disappear just by lying on my back.' She was thoughtful for a while, and then she reverted to their previous conversation, and said, 'I think you should be famous.'

'Why?'

'Because you're so good on the piano and in bed. At least, I seem to remember that you are. Maybe I need a reminder.'

'But you haven't got a piano here.'

'In that case, we'll just have to do it in bed.'

27

Gavin sat in his office, going minutely through the score of *Royal Rivals* He had to be absolutely sure it was right before the rehearsal at 5:15.

There was a knock on the door.

'Come in.'

The door opened. It was Leah.

He asked, 'How did the assessment go?'

'Remarkably well. Dawn did exceptionally well, but I expected her to. She's quite outstanding.'

'Pretty, too.'

Leah waved an admonishing finger. 'She's only twenty.'

'Is that all? Anyway, I'm rather keen on her teacher.'

'So I gather.'

'What did the assessors say?'

'They were impressed too. They were very interested in the show as well.'

'Let's hope it lives up to expectations.'

A week of rehearsals followed, after which Vincent, Leah and Gavin were confident that the cast and orchestra were prepared and that little more could be done to make the show a success. The hotel had been booked at an earlier date and the coaches were ordered. It seemed that everything was going as planned, and then a student arrived at Leah's office in a state of anxiety.

'Leah,' she said, 'can I speak to you?'

Leah laid down her pen. 'Of course you may. What is it?'

'It's Dawn. She's sprained her ankle. She's in the Refectory.'

'What happened?'

'She was running and she fell on her ankle. That's all I know.'

Leah picked up her keys and headed for the Refectory, arriving at the same time as Vincent, who had also heard about the incident.

Dawn sat on a plastic dining chair, tearful and in obvious pain. Her ankle was very swollen.

'She must have it X-rayed,' said Vincent. 'We can't take any chances with an injury like this.'

'I'll take her,' said Leah. 'My car's at this end of the carpark.'

'Okay. Open up your car and I'll bring her across.'

Leah hurried over to her car, unlocking it and pushing the passenger seat back as far as it would go. Vincent arrived, carrying Dawn in his arms. 'It was easier than helping her across,' he said.

'Thanks, Vincent. Dawn, do you live locally or are you in digs?'

'I live in Knaresborough,' she said, wincing with pain.

'Leave it with me,' said Vincent. 'I'll phone Dawn's home.'

As Leah drove off, Dawn said, 'I'm going to miss the show, aren't I?'

'We don't know yet. We'll have a better idea after the X-ray.' As she spoke, she had a pretty good idea that Dawn was right. For the moment, however, the girl was emotionally vulnerable as well as injured, and she needed gentle handling.

They reached the hospital fairly quickly and, as Leah helped Dawn into a wheelchair, an officious man in an anonymous uniform said, 'You can't leave your car there.'

Controlling her impatience, Leah said, 'I'll come back and move it when I've got this patient into Casualty.'

She followed the arrows that led to the Casualty Department and found Reception. 'Give your name and details to the receptionist, Dawn,' she said, 'and I'll be back when I've parked my car.'

When she reached her car, she found the same official close by, but drove away without speaking to him. There was nothing to be gained through unpleasantness. She parked the car and returned to Casualty, where Dawn had given her details to the receptionist and was waiting to be seen. She was still tearful, although Leah imagined that had more to do with the likelihood of missing the show than with shock and pain. In the absence of anything useful to say, she took her hand to give her what comfort she could.

Dawn said again, 'I'm going to miss the show, aren't I?'

'Wait until they've done the X-ray,' Leah told her. 'Then we'll know.'

'I couldn't bear to miss it.'

'I know.' No stranger to disappointment, Leah could only sympathise.

Eventually, a nurse called out, 'Dawn Thompson.'

'Here.' Leah pushed the wheelchair through the open doorway to a room with several bays.

'Over here,' said the nurse, indicating one of the bays, where a man in a white coat, presumably a doctor, sat at a desk. 'Injured right ankle,' the nurse told the doctor.

'Can we get the shoe off?'

It was a delicate procedure, and Leah held Dawn's hand firmly while the nurse removed the shoe, because it was clearly agonising.

'We're going to need an X-ray,' said the doctor after a cursory examination.

'Right, Doctor, I'll get someone to take her to X-ray.'

Leah asked, 'Will I be allowed to go with her? She has no one else until one of her family arrives.'

'In that case, yes,' said the doctor. He wrote something on a form, presumably an X-ray request, and handed it to the nurse, who went in search of a porter.

They returned, eventually, from X-ray, and the nurse called again for Dawn. Leah wheeled her through, by this time all-but re-signed to Dawn missing the show.

The doctor examined the X-ray, and said, 'There's no fracture, but you've probably torn a ligament. We'll give you an ice pack to reduce the swelling, and then you'll have to keep it bandaged for two to three weeks.'

Dawn's reaction was a howl of anguish followed by great, shaking sobs. Leah put her arm around her, squeezing her shoulder in helpless sympathy.

Somewhat surprised, the doctor said, 'Take heart. It's not the end of the world, you know.'

'It probably feels like it,' said Leah. 'She was going to dance in a show, next weekend, in a London theatre.'

'Oh, I'm sorry. I'd no idea.'

They waited while the nurse produced an ice-pack.

'There,' she said. 'We'll leave it like that for a while before we dress it for you.'

After a while, Dawn, who had been crying silently, suddenly looked up as someone came into the waiting area. 'Mum,' she wailed, breaking into another paroxysm of sobs.

'Oh, Dawn,' said her mother, crouching beside the wheelchair and taking her daughter in her arms, 'what have you been up to?'

'I'm Leah Hinchcliffe,' said Leah.

'How do you do, Miss Hinchcliffe? Dawn's told me a lot about you. Thank you for bringing her.'

'It was no trouble.' She got up to leave, but then joined Dawn's mother in crouching beside the chair. 'Dawn, you won't think so now, but you'll get over this. I can tell you that from experience. You've lost an opportunity to dance in a show, but I lost my dancing career. Believe me, I know how it feels when fate plays a rotten trick on you.'

Dawn's expression confirmed her disbelief.

'I want you to come to London, Dawn. Join the others in the dressing room, and then watch the whole thing from the wings, because you're still a part of it. You're one of the cast, even with your ankle in a bandage.' As she stood up to leave, she said, 'With your talent, you'll go on to much greater things. You'll see.'

~·⚙·~

When she returned to the college, she found Vincent watching the rehearsal. He motioned to her to step outside the hall.

'It's a torn ligament,' she told him. 'She won't be allowed to dance for several weeks.'

'Poor girl. She must be heartbroken.'

'Devastated,' she confirmed.

'And you can't be feeling too good about it either.'

'Is it so obvious, Vincent?'

191

'No, but I know you well enough.'

'It's a Hinchcliffe characteristic, I'm afraid.'

'It's an awful thing to happen to her, and so close to the performance.'

Leah remembered what she'd said to Dawn prior to leaving her at the hospital. 'I've told her I want her to come with us,' she said. 'That way, she'll still feel that she's part of the show.'

It seemed to set Vincent thinking. 'We need a prompt,' he said.

'She could do that easily from a chair in the wings.'

'Right, I'll offer her that.' He thought again and said, 'I suppose it's too late to give the part to someone else.'

'No one else could dance it as well as Dawn, and it's too late anyway.'

Vincent nodded gravely. 'It's the greatest pity, but we'll just have to scrap the ballet scene.'

'Unless....'

'What, Leah?'

'No, it would look like the worst kind of self-indulgence.'

'No, it wouldn't. It would look like you saving the scene. That's if we're thinking along the same lines.'

'All right,' she said, 'I'll dance the scene.'

28

LONDON

After a successful dress rehearsal, Leah, Gavin and Vincent took their leave of the TV crew, who were setting up their cameras, and shepherded the students back to the hotel for a meal before the performance. Leah was surprised to see her parents in the lobby.

'Hello,' she said, greeting each of them with a kiss. 'Are you staying here as well?'

'No,' said her mum, 'we couldn't get in here. We're staying at the Strand Palace Hotel.'

'You'll come back for the after-show party, I hope?'

'Yes, we'll look in.'

'Especially now that we know you're going to be dancing.'

'It's just a small part near the end, Dad.'

'Even so.'

'Where's Gavin?'

'He's gone to find his clarinet teacher, Mum, the one who played with the dance bands before the war.'

'I'd like to meet him.'

'You will, Dad. He's coming to the party.'

'We're going back to our hotel now, to eat, but we'll see you later on.'

'Okay, Mum.'

'Break a leg, darling.'

Leah winced at the thought of Dawn's ankle. 'Thanks, Mum. Enjoy the show.'

She was about to go in search of Gavin, when she spotted another face she knew. 'Neil,' she said. 'We weren't expecting you.'

'I had to come, darling. After all, I wrote most of the bloody thing. I see the play is down on the programme as "Book by Neil Quarmby. Final Scene by Vincent Palmer". I suppose I'll be haunted by that for the rest of my career.'

'Very likely, Neil, and it's no one's fault but yours. You'll have to excuse me.'

'I have to go, too. I couldn't get a room in this bloody hotel.'

It was as well. Negative influences had no place at a pre-performance gathering. Leah looked again for Gavin and found him in conversation with Frank Morrison and a middle-aged couple.

'Leah,' said Gavin, 'come and meet Mr and Mrs Hutchins. You know Frank, of course.'

Leah shook hands with Mr and Mrs Hutchins, who told her to call them 'Hutch' and 'Ellie'. Ellie was a very attractive woman, who spoke with no discernible accent. Her husband, on the other hand, was unmistakably a son of the West Riding. His fair, greying hair was combed into an immaculate centre parting.

'I'm very proud of Gavin,' he told her. 'In fact, I'm proud of both of these lads, and we're all looking forward to tonight's performance.'

'My dad can't wait to meet you, Hutch. He's had a dance band in Wensleydale since he came home from the war. He says he's fighting a one-man rear-guard action to save the music of the golden era.'

'In that case, I have to meet him, Leah.'

Ellie said, 'Gavin tells me you're dancing tonight, Leah.'

'Only because one of the girls is injured. I wouldn't do it otherwise.'

'I think everyone must realise that.'

'There's a terrific buzz tonight,' said Frank, speaking for the first time. 'I imagine the students have all got butterflies, but they're excited as well.'

Vincent's voice came over the address system. 'Good evening ladies and gentlemen, and welcome to this performance of *Royal Rivals*. I have to announce that Dawn Thompson is indisposed, and

194

that the part of Lady Jane Grey will be danced by Leah Hinchcliffe.'

In the wings, Leah gave Dawn a sympathetic hug before checking that the Beginners were in place behind the curtain. There was a roll on the bass drum, and the overture, a *pot pourri* of themes from the show, began. For herself, Leah had no nerves, at least for the time being. The tension she felt was for the students.

The overture ended, and as the next number began, the curtain rose to reveal a number of monarchs gathered in twos and threes. On a spotlight cue, the first one, a medieval-looking character, said, 'Six hundred years within these walls.' Another said, 'And I for a century more.'

The next said, 'For me, three hundred, and the prospect palls.' Finally, 'Must we haunt the Lower Chambers evermore?'

The dialogue passed between the four groups again, and then there was a trumpet fanfare followed by an announcement over the address system.

'Due to a hard-hitting piece of investigative journalism, a hero has been debunked, and there is now a vacancy in the Upper Chambers. The Supreme Council has decided that it is the turn of the royal personages to compete for election. Proposals may now be submitted.'

There was another fanfare amid cheers and shouts of excitement, as the company came on stage, and the orchestra started the introduction to the opening chorus. After sixteen bars, binoculars appeared, tic-tac signals were being made, and the runners appeared upstage, moving in slow motion.

'The going's firm, and everywhere there's nervous expectation. All bets are off, the viewers sense the punters' trepidation.' Here, TV cameras appeared above the chorus, greeted by laughter from the audience. The ice had been broken.

As the chorus ended, the stage was darkened behind the gauze as King Philip the Second of Spain made his entrance. The character appeared nervous, looking to left and right, and finally addressing the audience to ask why he should be the object of censure simply because of his absorbing pastime, namely torturing.

The gauze was lifted and the upstage area was lighted to reveal a torture chamber in which long-dead victims, now skeletons, hung from chains. As the introduction was played, the victims came to life, moving to the rhythm, and when King Philip sang his chorus, they danced the Charleston to the audience's obvious delight. At the end, applause was fierce, and Angus was able to perform his rehearsed encore.

A chorus and two of Leah's favourite numbers came next. Michael made an excellent job of his Country and Western song as Edward the Seventh, and the remainder of the first half seemed to take no time at all. At the interval, Leah met Gavin backstage.

'There's a buzz from the audience,' she said. 'You can hear it now.'

'That's the impression I'm getting,' he said, crossing his fingers. 'So far, so good. How's Dawn?'

'She's concentrating like mad on the script. It's been the perfect diversion for her.'

'Good.'

'You look good in white tie and tails,' she observed.

'It's just as well. I've got a date with a ballerina tonight, and she's something special, so I have to dress appropriately.'

'Special?'

'I think so.'

'I think you're rather special too.' She kissed him hurriedly. 'I'll see you later. I have to go to the dressing rooms.'

She knocked on the ladies' dressing room door and said, 'Girls, it's Leah.'

Someone said, 'Come in, Leah.'

They were all changed for their next number. They stopped whatever they were doing to listen to her.

'Girls, you've been brilliant. Keep it up!'

One of them said, 'It'll be your turn soon, Leah.'

'Don't. You'll make me nervous.'

They laughed. It was a good sign, so she went to the men's changing room. 'Boys, are you all decent? It's Leah.'

She left them with the same message and returned to stand beside Dawn in the wings.

After the first chorus of the second half, the five wives of Henry the Eighth entered, explaining bitchily to the audience why the sixth was absent. Then they delivered their song, alternating decorum with bawdiness, so that the audience called them back for their rehearsed encore.

The cast performed number after number seamlessly and with total commitment, and the chorus were equally excellent. Eventually, the time came for Leah to change for the last scene. Suddenly, she was nervous at the realisation that she was about to perform. As she dressed in Jane's hastily-altered ballet costume, however, she reminded herself that a company of inexperienced students were making a magnificent job of entertaining a London audience, and that humbling thought calmed her.

She re-joined Dawn in the wings two numbers before the scene, and whispered, 'How's it going?'

Dawn simply nodded, concentrating as hard as ever on the script.

Eventually, the gauze and the lights came down, the headsman's block was put into place and, downstage, Lady Jane was led into the Council Chamber. Leah turned to the dancers and nodded. Silently, they positioned themselves ready for their entrance behind the gauze.

Jane sang, 'I am the forgotten queen, once crowned but lost in history.'

The atmosphere in the theatre was intense.

'Who forced you, Jane?' The Chairman's voice was authoritative but gentle.

'My father, sir, though I am ashamed to say it, and my father-in-law, the Duke of Northumberland.'

By this time, Leah reckoned that every member of the audience must be rooting for Jane.

Her song continued. 'In my childlike purpose, I would see myself erase,

The state of moral poverty that men would fain embrace.

With will, such deeds would flourish in time, and with goodwill,

But time was then denied me, and kindness was there nil.'

Jane knelt before the Council, the upstage lights came up and Leah, as Jane's other self was led slowly to the place of execution, looking around her for the last time. It felt strange, dancing her own choreography, but she put that thought out of her mind and concentrated on the dance itself.

In compliance with Jane's request, she was blindfolded, allowed to feel her way, at first without success, and then guided and supported elaborately to the block, where she knelt in an attitude of prayer.

The headsman raised his axe, and the lights came slowly down. The Chairman spoke again to Jane.

'Why was it so important for you to instruct the nation, Jane?'

'Learning gave me pleasure, sir. Why should it not do as much for the people? Is it not also true that learning is the most civilising influence?'

Leah could hear audience members sniffing behind their tissues as the Chairman said, 'Let us return, for the moment, to the beginning of your testimony, when you told us that you pleaded Mary's right to the throne. Why did you do that?'

'She was the true heiress, sir, the child of Henry and Katherine.'

'But she was a Catholic and you were a Protestant.'

''Tis true, sir. I had no love for her chosen path, but she was, even so, the rightful heiress.'

'But she had you beheaded for treason.'

'That is also true, sir.'

'What are your feelings towards Mary Tudor, Jane?'

There was a meaningful silence, and then Jane answered, 'Sir, I forgive her.'

Gavin brought up the volume for the final four bars, and the audience burst into spontaneous if premature applause.

All that remained was for the Chairman to announce the Council's decision, that Queen Jane the First, formerly Lady Jane Grey, was to be elevated to the Upper Chambers.

There was greater applause, during which Leah and the dancers exited the stage so that the chorus could make its entrance for the Finale.

Dawn's cheeks were wet.

'Remember,' Leah told her, giving her an encouraging hug, 'you're still one of the company.'

'That's not why I'm crying, Leah. It was you. You were beautiful.'

'Thank you, Dawn.'

Curtain calls followed, and Leah appeared in costume with the rest. When everyone, including Neil, Vincent, Gavin and the orchestra had been acknowledged, Leah walked into the wings and returned with Dawn on her crutches, to take her applause.

By the time Leah arrived at the hotel, her parents, Martin and Wendy were there to welcome her.

'Well done, darling,' said her mum, looking quite emotional.

Her dad was less so, but equally delighted with his daughter. Even Martin expressed his admiration. Wendy, whose make-up showed signs of recent repair, said, 'I cried all through that last bit, Leah. You were wonderful!'

Leah saw Hutch and Ellie approaching. 'Dad,' she said, 'I want you to meet—'

'We've already met, love. We're staying in the same hotel.'

Hutch and Ellie congratulated her.

'It was only a tiny part,' she protested.

'And beautifully danced,' said her mum.

'Well done, Leah,' said Gavin suddenly appearing. 'Folks, I want you to meet my mum, Graham and Uncle Stan.' Frank arrived then, and joined in their congratulations.

They chatted until three more of the party joined the crowd.

'There was a queue for the ladies' room,' said Elaine. 'It was getting quite urgent for Janice.'

'The scene wasn't that funny,' said Leah.

'No.' Janice was quick to enlighten her. 'I just needed to do a—'

'I think we can take that as read,' said Bailey, 'whereas credit must go where it's due. Congratulations, Leah and Gavin, on a masterpiece! Now, let's get some drinks in.'

Much later, Leah and Gavin lay together in post-coital peace and contentment.

'There,' he said, 'I told you it was possible to do it without Granados playing in the background.'

'It's surprising what skills you can acquire when the chips are down.' Turning to face him, she asked, 'Did he write more pieces like that?'

'Oh, yes. "Colloquio", the piece you know, is from "Goyescas", sometimes called "Young Men in Love". There are five other pieces. There's "Flattery", "The Fandango by Lamplight", "The Maiden and the Nightingale", "Love and Death" and "Epilogue".'

'Will you record one of them for me when we get back?'

'Now the show's out of the way, it'll be a pleasure.'

'I realise,' she said, settling back into her pillows, 'that I know very little about music.'

'I don't know the first thing about ballet,' said Gavin, 'but I thought you were incredible tonight.'

'Thank you, but you would say that, wouldn't you?'

'Yes, but hand on heart, you know.'

'I know. Thank you.'

They lay in companionable silence, until Leah said, 'Hey, I'm really taken with your Uncle Stan. He's just as I imagined: ample, cheery and full of goodwill.'

'That's him,' agreed Gavin.

'There was a lot of good feeling around tonight. There were some people here from the East Lancashire Academy. They really enjoyed the show.'

'Let's hope a lot of potential students will when the programme goes out.'

29

Three weeks after the show, the Principal called an end-of-day meeting of all staff in the Recital Hall.

'As you all know,' he said when everyone was settled, 'this college has been under severe financial pressure for some time. You also know that the two schools recently mounted a production in London's West End, in a praiseworthy bid to attract more students to the college. With more time, it might easily have done the trick. However, time was a luxury we were not allowed.' He held up one hand as the murmuring in the hall grew louder. 'I have to tell you, then, that this college will close at the end of June and reopen in September as part of The Northern College of Performance Arts.'

The murmur stopped for the moment, as everyone waited to hear the detail.

'This is the result of a merger with Dunelm College of Theatre Arts.' The noise recommenced, and the Principal held up his hands once more. 'Students will return in the normal way, in September, and their studies should not be affected unduly by the transition.' He took a breath and summoned his resolve to deliver his final message. 'I shall be taking premature retirement. I regret to say, however, that academic, administrative and ancillary staff will be required to reapply for their posts. Details will be circulated within the week, as time is short.'

Making her way past other stunned and devastated members of staff, Leah eventually found Gavin, Vincent and Neil.

'Hands up all those who feel completely flattened,' she said.

'I feel betrayed,' said Neil, adding pointedly, 'although I have to say, not for the first time.' He turned his back on them and headed for the carpark.

'That was opportune,' said Vincent, watching him go. 'Yes, this has come as a shock to everyone. They must have been negotiating the merger while we were preparing for the show.'

'After all the work the students put in,' said Leah, 'not to mention Gavin's musical marathon and, although it pains me to mention it, Neil's script.' She added quickly, 'And your rescue work towards the end, Vincent.' She flung out her arms in a gesture of hopelessness. 'Everyone had built up their hopes, and now they're shattered. It's just too cruel for words.' Blinking repeatedly, she said, 'At least the students will still have their places. It's just a pity for them that they don't know yet who's going to teach them.'

Gavin said, 'I'd better go before someone calls me "Jonah". This is the second time in a year I've been in a similar situation. The only difference this time is the option to reapply.'

'Don't go yet, at least for a minute, Gavin,' said Vincent.

Leah asked, 'Why did you call Neil's flouncing exit "opportune"?'

'There are things I need to tell you that I don't want made public.' Vincent looked round to make sure he couldn't be overheard. 'The Principal isn't the only one who's leaving,' he said. 'I put my resignation in at Christmas. I didn't tell you, because the last thing you both needed to hear was that I was leaving the sinking ship.'

'Where are you going?' Leah's question was one of innocent enquiry.

'East Lancashire Academy. It's a sideways move but a welcome one.'

'Congratulations, Vincent,' said Gavin. 'You deserve it.'

'I couldn't agree more,' said Leah.

'Thank you, both, but now, not surprisingly, you're each concerned about your future.'

Their solemn faces confirmed it.

'The best advice I can offer at this stage is to keep a close eye on your pigeonholes.'

Both Leah and Gavin had been puzzled by Vincent's cryptic suggestion, but they accepted it all the same, and Leah was rewarded two weeks later, when she received a letter from an unexpected source. At the end of the day, which was her first opportunity, she found Gavin in his office.

'I got this letter this morning,' she told him.

'That's a coincidence. This came today.' He picked up a letter from his 'Do' tray. 'What does yours say?'

'First, I want to know what yours says.'

'All right. I'll show you mine if you'll show me yours.'

'All right.'

They exchanged letters. Both were from the East Lancashire Academy of Performing Arts and, in each case, a post description was enclosed.

Leah read, *Dear Mr Lowe,*

We were regrettably unable to fill the previously advertised post of Senior Lecturer in Music, and we are therefore obliged to re-advertise it, and we would welcome expressions of interest. The starting date would be ideally September 1976, although we would naturally honour contractual commitments. A description of the post is enclosed.

She looked at the description and read aloud, 'The successful candidate will assume responsibility for courses in Conducting and Composition as well as offering an instrument, preferably Piano. An additional responsibility will be that of close co-operation with the School of Drama and Dance.' She dropped the letter in his tray and said, 'I know what mine says, because I've read it.'

'Wait. I'm still reading it.' He looked down again. 'It's come about due to expansion, which is always good to hear. Ballet is an essential discipline, although there will be some Jazz as well.' He handed it back to her. 'What does this mean, Leah?'

'It means we're being headhunted an' all that jazz, and I must say, it's in the nick of time.'

'I agree, and speaking of time,' said Gavin, consulting his watch, 'do you fancy a drink?'

'I think that would be an excellent idea.' She waited until he was clear of his desk, before throwing her arms round his neck. 'You and me,' she exulted, 'at East Lancashire Academy!' They celebrated discreetly before leaving the campus in a calm and professional manner.

As they walked sensibly to the pub, Gavin said, 'Are you sure it means they're headhunting us?'

'That's what the magic words "we would welcome expressions of interest" usually mean.'

'It's quite a coincidence that they wrote to both of us at the same time.'

'Vincent invited them to the show. For my money, this is his doing. He wanted them to see what we could do.'

'And it keeps us together.' They walked a little further, and he said, 'You know, walking along like this after all the recent excitement reminds me of that line everybody quotes from the end of *Casablanca*.'

'I know, when Claude Rains says, "This could be the start of a beautiful friendship." But it started some time ago, and I hope it's going to be much more than a friendship.'

'It already is. At least, from my point of view.'

'Mine too,' she agreed. 'How could it be otherwise?' She took his arm in the way that had become familiar. 'If everything goes according to plan,' she said thoughtfully, 'we'll have to find fresh accommodation.'

'True.'

'I suppose we could always simplify the process.'

'How would we do that?'

Lowering her voice quite unnecessarily, she explained, 'By living in sin.'

'The prospect grows more inviting by the second.'

'But, for the time being, and I'm thinking about tonight....'

'Yes?'

'Your place or mine?'

THE END

Lightning Source UK Ltd.
Milton Keynes UK
UKHW041142110222
398418UK00006B/5